TRUE TENCHI MUYO!

VOLUME 2

YOSHO

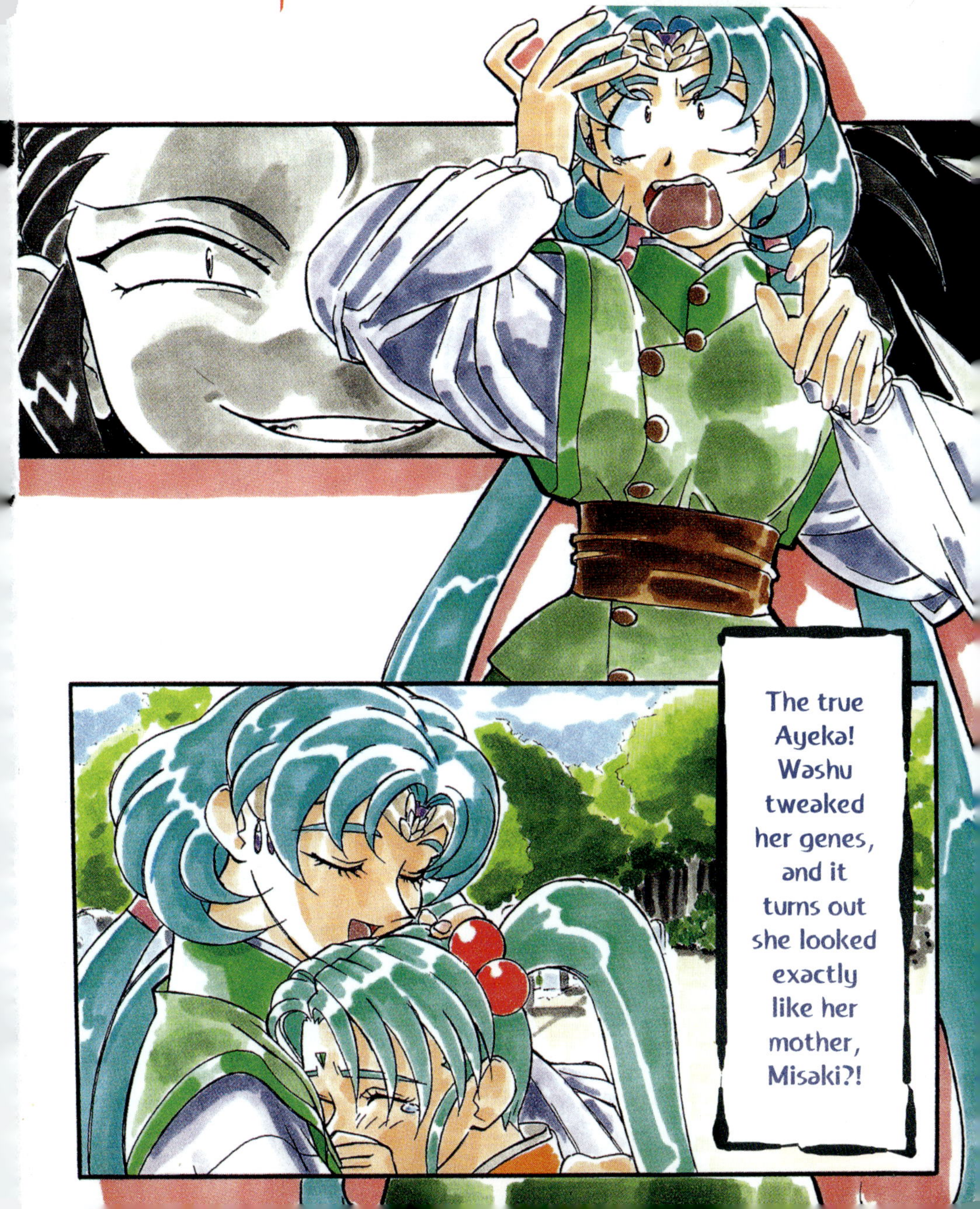
The true Ayeka! Washu tweaked her genes, and it turns out she looked exactly like her mother, Misaki?!

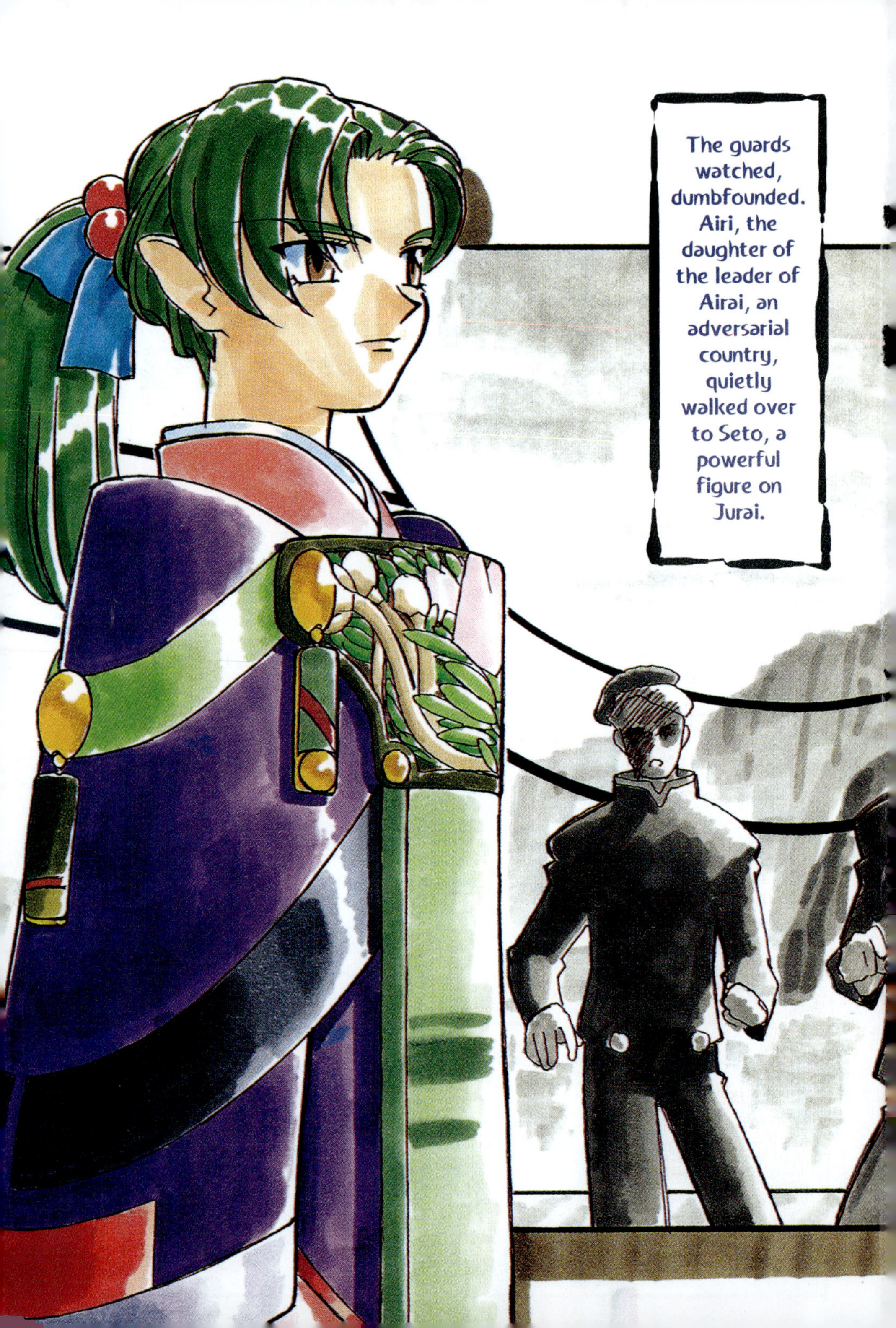
The guards watched, dumbfounded. Airi, the daughter of the leader of Airai, an adversarial country, quietly walked over to Seto, a powerful figure on Jurai.

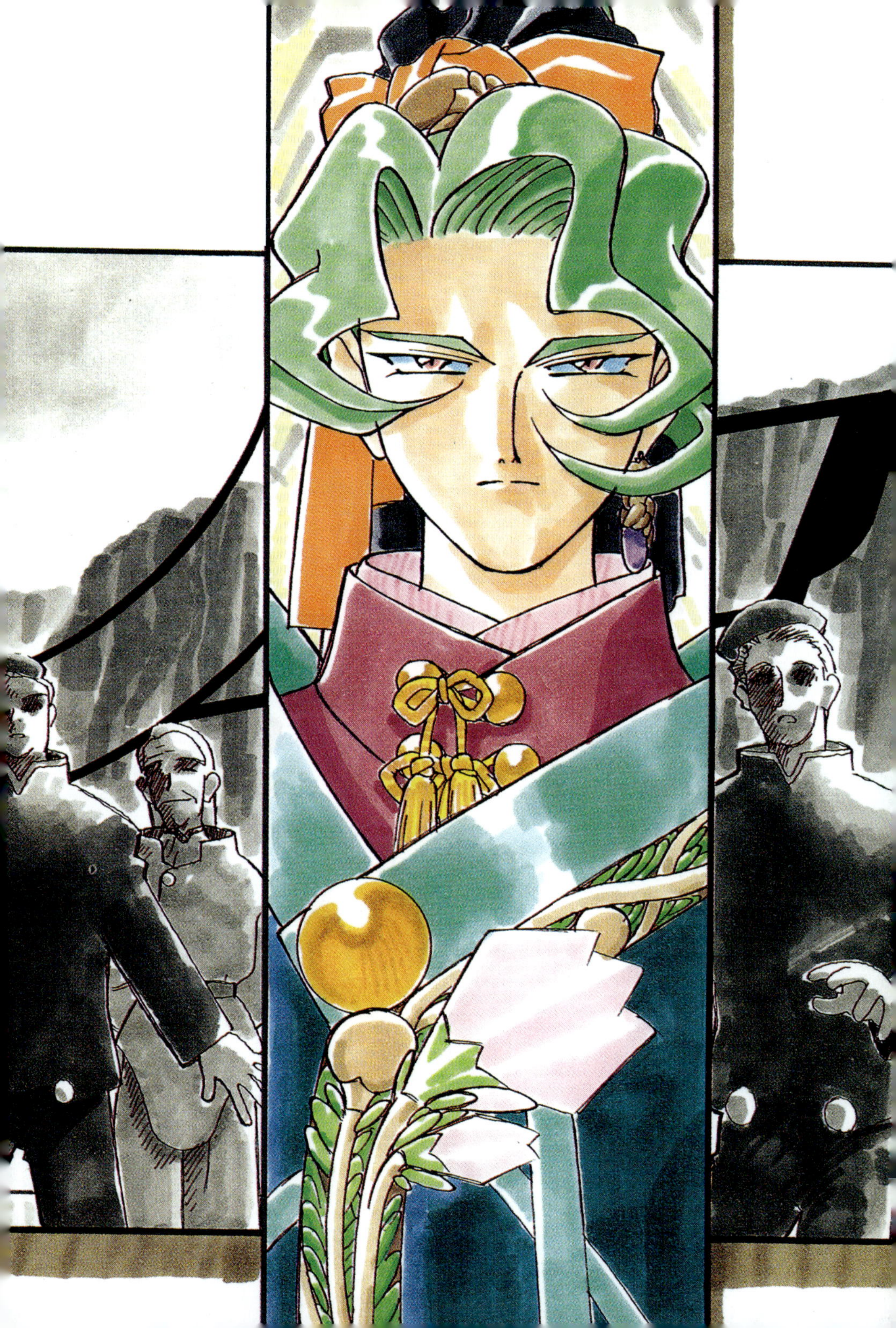

"I'm Mizuho, your daughter!"
Yosho's mind went blank at the shocking truth from which he had been kept in the dark for several hundred years.

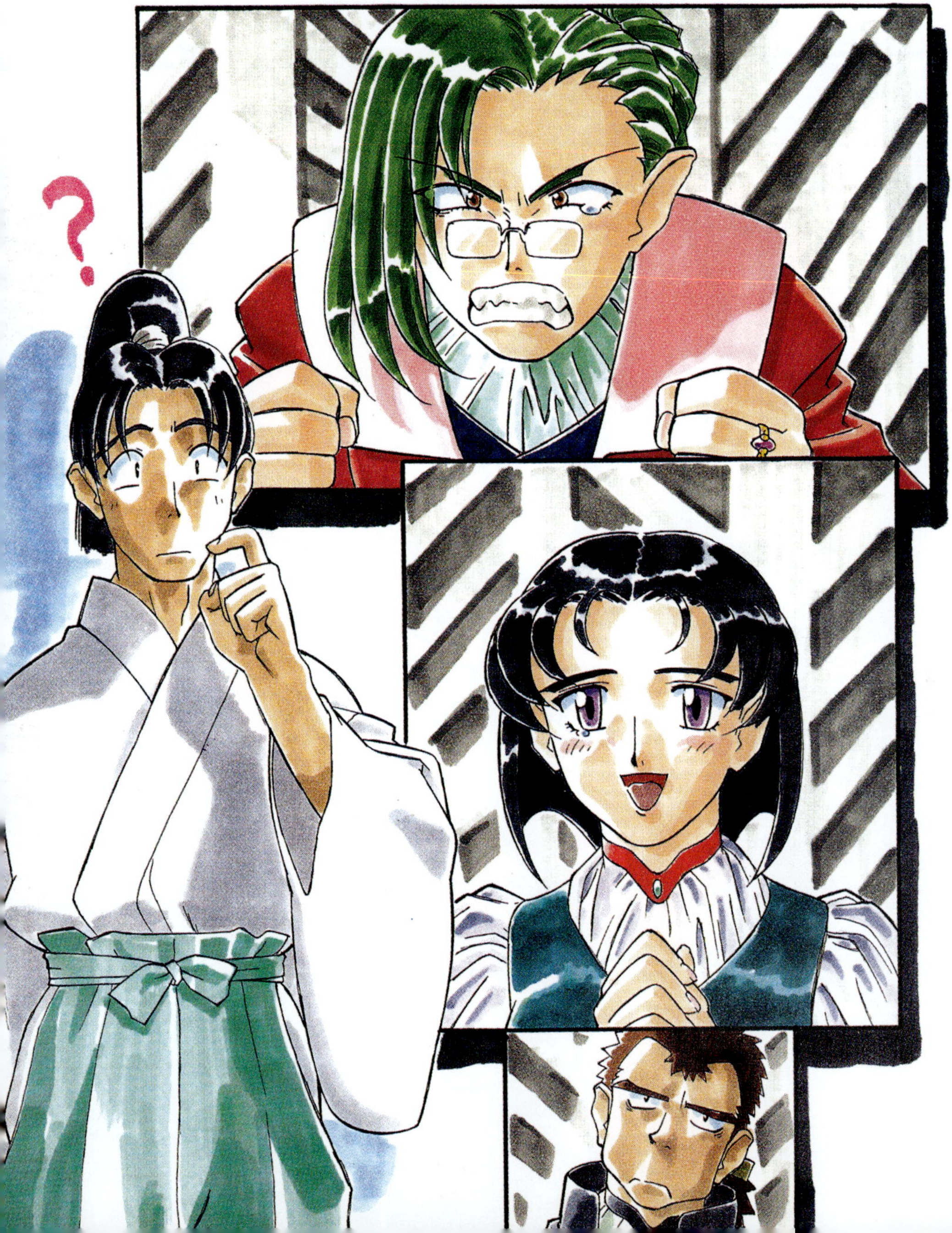
?

TRUE TENCHI MUYO!

VOLUME 2
YOSHO

BY

Yousuke Kuroda &
Masaki Kajishima

Seven Seas

Seven Seas Entertainment

SHIN TENCHIMUYO! RYO O KI Vol. 2 YOSHO

© Yousuke Kuroda, Masaki Kajishima 1998
© AIC/PIONEER LDC.

First published in Japan in 1998 by KADOKAWA CORPORATION, Tokyo. English translation rights arranged with KADOKAWA CORPORATION, Tokyo.

No portion of this book may be reproduced or transmitted in any form without written permission from the copyright holders. This is is a work of fiction. Names, characters, places, and incidents are the products of the author's imagination or are used fictitiously. Any resemblance to actual events, locales, or persons, living or dead, is entirely coincidental.

Seven Seas books may be purchased in bulk for promotional, educational, or business use. Please contact your local bookseller or the Macmillan Corporate and Premium Sales Department at 1-800-221-7945, extension 5442, or by e-mail at MacmillanSpecialMarkets@macmillan.com.

Seven Seas and the Seven Seas logo are trademarks of Seven Seas Entertainment, LLC. All rights reserved.

Follow Seven Seas Entertainment online at sevenseasentertainment.com.

TRANSLATION: Lillian Olsen
ADAPTATION: AstroNerdBoy
COVER DESIGN: Nicky Lim
INTERIOR LAYOUT & DESIGN: Clay Gardner
PROOFREADER: Jade Gardner, Dayna Abel
ASSISTANT EDITOR: Jenn Grunigen
LIGHT NOVEL EDITOR: Nibedita Sen
DIGITAL MANAGER: CK Russell
EDITOR-IN-CHIEF: Adam Arnold
PUBLISHER: Jason DeAngelis

ISBN: 978-1-626926-17-2
Printed in Canada
First Printing: June 2018
10 9 8 7 6 5 4 3 2 1

Table of Contents

PROLOGUE	*9*
AYEKA	*19*
YOSHO	*37*
AIRI	*59*
PUPPY FUNAHO	*91*
KANEMITSU	*117*
AIRI AGAIN	*135*
SETO AND AIRI	*149*
RYOKO'S ATTACK	*169*
AZUSA	*203*
EPILOGUE	*225*
AFTERWORD	*235*
CHARACTER SHEETS	*239*

Prologue

It was late may. The sun's rays occasionally hinted at the summer to come. The Emperor of Jurai and his entourage had gone home at last, and the Masaki household, released from the daily cacophony, was awash in an almost desolate silence. Sasami, cradling Ryo-Ohki (who was in beast mode), let out a deep sigh.

"Mew?" Ryo-Ohki, concerned, turned up to look at Sasami with those impossibly adorable round eyes. Those were the eyes that any animal lover would squeal at and have to resist the urge to hug tightly and wouldn't be able to help but nuzzle in the end.

Sasami patted Ryo-Ohki's head reassuringly and let her eyes wander towards Okayama's nature-rich countryside. The few hours between cleaning up from lunch and starting preparations for dinner were Sasami's free time. She would usually read some shoujo manga or leisurely bask in a sunbeam with Ryo-Ohki, but having gotten used to the ruckus that had persisted until just a few days ago, Sasami could not settle down and sit still.

"Shall we go for a walk, Ryo-chan?"

"Meow!"

Ten or so minutes later, Sasami was busily cleaning the Masaki Shrine. The amount of energy a child running around the fields all day had was higher than you might think, and doing housework was not enough to use up that energy. The others helped out here and there, and Sasami was always diligent in keeping the place tidy, so she did not need as much time to do the housework. The boisterous merrymaking of just a few days ago had kept her running around so much that she was stuck in hyper housework mode, and now felt she had to be doing more, even though it was no longer necessary.

They had intended on a leisurely walk, but the weeds peeking up a few millimeters too long off the grounds of the shrine where Tenchi's grandfather lived bothered her; she plucked one and then another, and pretty soon she was cleaning the whole place. Humanoid-mode Ryo-Ohki, accompanying her on the walk, was helping out.

"Mew?" Suddenly noticing a swallowtail butterfly flitting about, she chased it as a toddler would. Her catlike qualities kept her focused solely on the butterfly, and she sailed over the grass and rolled down the slope... But this was a common occurrence, and her lively meowing could be heard from below to signal that she was okay.

Sasami sighed loudly again. Mihoshi had cleaned the shrine the previous day, so Sasami was quickly left with nothing to do. It might be surprising that Mihoshi was very good with housework. It just took her a loooong time... Sasami sighed yet again.

PROLOGUE

"What's wrong, Sasami-chan?" It was Washu who spoke to Sasami, who was noticeably lacking her usual sunny demeanor.

"Waaaaaaaaaaaaah!" Eyes open wide, Sasami's scream echoed through the mountains.

"Sasami, what's the matter?!" Katsuhito dashed out from the shrine office, for Sasami hardly ever screamed like that. Ryo-Ohki scrambled up a moment behind him. However, they both pulled up short, as they understood everything in just one glance. "Hm... I see."

"Meow."

Washu, with soot on her face and a spider web draped across her head, had stuck her upper body out from under the deck of the main shrine. "Sticking out from under the floors looking like that... shock is an understandable reaction," Katsuhito muttered to Ryo-Ohki, watching Washu's eccentric behavior. Ryo-Ohki meowed in agreement.

Meanwhile, Washu, still peering from below Sasami's feet, asked "Did I surprise you, Sasami?!" in her usual cheerful way, paying no heed to how she looked or to Sasami's expression of shock.

"W-Washu-oneechan...why are you..." She tried to ask what she was doing there and stopped short. Knowing Washu, she was hunting for ingredients to use in her experiments, of course. In point of fact, she was observing the doodlebug constructing a nest in the dry, fine sand under the shrine. Nobody knew what she would do with those observations, however...

Washu chuckled innocently at Sasami. That was all it took for Sasami—or anyone who knew Washu, for that matter—to *know* that she was up to no good.

I hope Tenchi-oniichan, Ryoko-oneechan, and Ayeka-oneesama are safe, Sasami prayed silently to herself.

"Something on your mind? Other than the thing about Tenchi-dono and Ryoko-chan and Ayeka-dono you were thinking about just now. I'm talking about why you were sighing."

"It's nothing. I was just hoping that everyone made it back to Jurai safely…"

Operation Arranged Marriage, where Azusa, the Emperor of Jurai, brought a suitor for Ayeka, the First Princess, to Earth to duel with Tenchi, had lasted ten days. They could no longer ignore their royal duties and had returned to their home world. But for Sasami, the Second Princess, it had meant spending time with her parents, which she hardly ever got to do. The bigger the ruckus over ten days, the bigger the hole it left in her heart. She may have been wise beyond her years, but she was still a child. Of course she was homesick.

Washu crawled out from under the crawl space, flicked off the dust particles, and drew Sasami closer into a hug.

She's so warm… Sasami was unconcerned about the soot and the dust. She felt a profound sense of relief. Washu's usual manner made her seem hard to approach, but she gave Sasami a feeling of peace.

"Say, Sasami…" Washu may have reminded Sasami of the Holy Mother, but once she realized that Sasami was calmer, she slipped back into her usual ways. "I was thinking, after meeting Misaki-dono, that Ayeka-dono looks a lot more like her mother than I thought."

"Ha ha...her personality, yes." Sasami laughed nervously. This topic was taboo in front of Ayeka, her older sister.

Washu chuckled, "Sasami, want me to show you something interesting?"

As soon as she said that, Sasami had a very bad feeling. The next moment, that feeling echoed in reality as the sound of Ayeka screaming rose from Tenchi's house.

"Ayeka-oneesama?!" Sasami immediately realized that Ayeka's scream must be caused by the "something interesting" Washu was talking about.

Soon, a dark and spiderlike object appeared on the shrine grounds. Ayeka was struggling, swallowed up within this black, viscous gel-like blob.

"Washu-oneechan!"

"It's okay!" Washu answered with her usual confident smile.

Knowing her, she wouldn't do anything too *unreasonable... I don't think...* Since the blob was opaque, Sasami could not see what kind of expression Ayeka had on her face. However, from the glimpse of her flailing legs, she could easily imagine. *I'm not sure about this...*

Ting! With the sound of a microwave's beep, the blob stopped moving.

"Looks like it's done... Observe."

Pushed lightly by Washu, Sasami stumbled towards Ayeka. The black blob separated. And from beneath it emerged...

"Ayeka-oneesa... A-Aye... Ayeka...onee...?" Sasami was shocked beyond words.

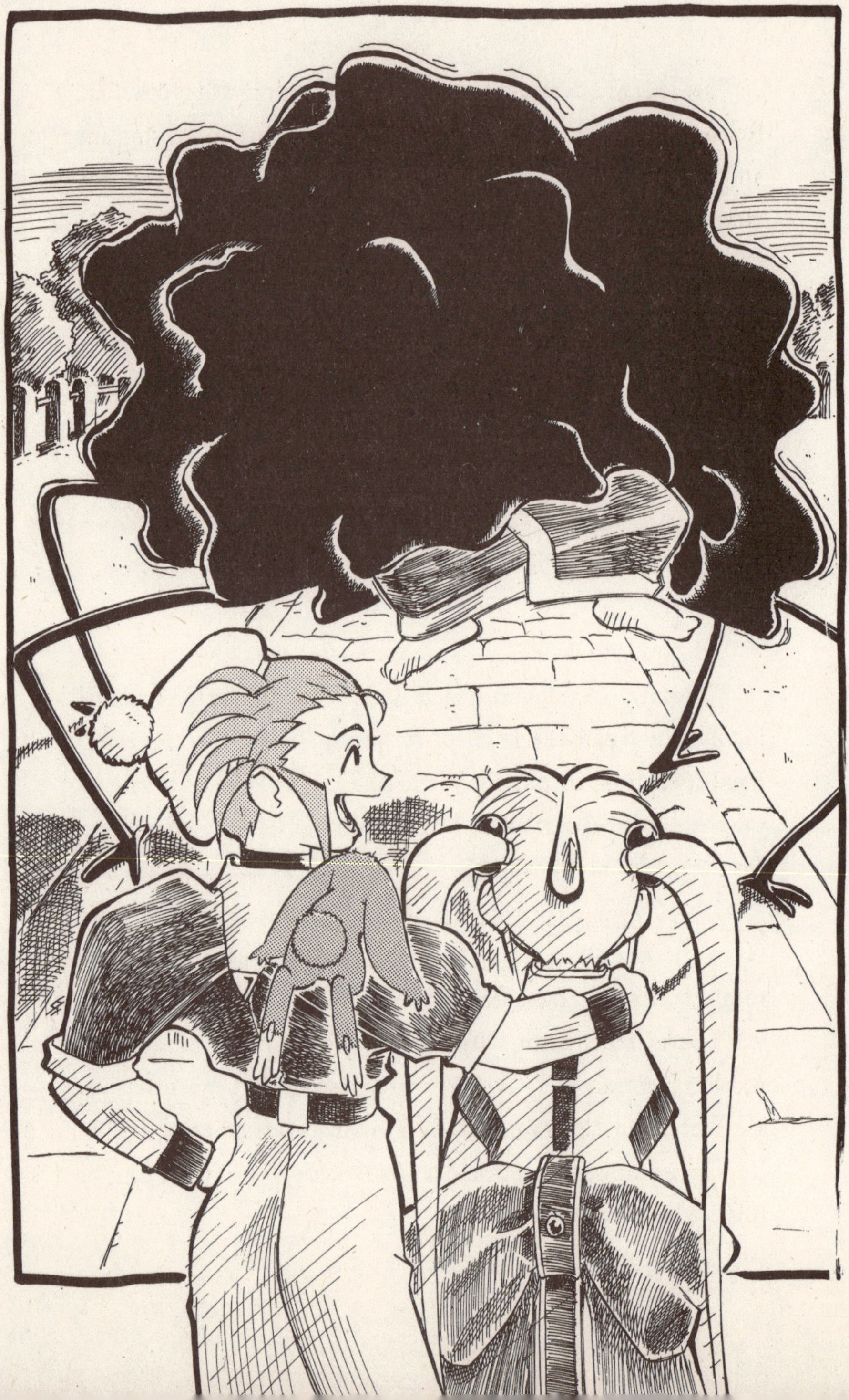

"Th-this was Washu-sama's doing, wasn't it?! What did she...?!" Released, Ayeka wore a complicated expression suppressing anger and glared at Washu. She was pretending to be okay, but it was clear she was infuriated.

"Your hair—exactly like mine and Mother's...?" Sasami mumbled, staring at Ayeka.

"What?" Ayeka patted her own hair and felt something different. She took out her hand mirror—a requisite for proper ladies—peered in, and two seconds later, screamed at the top of her lungs. The color of her hair had turned—or rather, *reverted* to a light blue-green, just like her mother Misaki's and Sasami's, and was spiky like a pineapple.

"Th-this hair is, um..." Ayeka tried to explain.

"Mother..." Sasami's voice cracked, and she clung to her sister.

"Sasami..." Ayeka finally realized that her little sister was lonely. She hardly ever relied on Ayeka since they had come to Earth. She took over most of the housework, and now that Ryo-Ohki was the baby of the house, Sasami was looking after her, too. Everyone around her, even her older sister, had forgotten that this brave little girl was only nine years old. "Sasami, you poor baby..." With a gentle smile, Ayeka lovingly squeezed Sasami. She had totally forgotten about her anger towards Washu. This simplicity was a part of the reason why she was often told she resembled her mother Misaki.

Watching the two sisters from the porch of the shrine, Katsuhito looked over at Washu. "Washu-dono, when did you notice that Ayeka had changed her hair?"

"Back when I did her physical examination." *Back then* was during the case of Ryoko-Zero. "Looking at her genes, it seemed her phenotype should more strongly resemble Misaki-dono, so I'd been wondering."

"When Ayeka was four...she underwent genetic editing." Katsuhito looked at Ayeka as he spoke. The color of her hair brought back old memories...of back when her hair was light blue-green. From the perspective of Earth, it was the far distant past. He remembered...back when he was still called Yosho...

Ayeka

Jurai, the empire with the largest territory in the universe, was a paradise of plants, covered in giant trees some thousand meters tall. Among them was an enormously large tree with a height of over five thousand meters. Its intricately layered branches were a habitat for countless species of plants and trees, and the foundation for urban structures. This aggregate was called Tenju, the Heaven's Tree.

Tenju was the capital of the planet of Jurai, the home of the Imperial Family, and its political and economic center. Of course, it had not grown naturally. It was carefully grown and cultivated over hundreds of thousands of years by the Royal Tree (Tsunami) and the Juraians. (Those with sharp tongues called it "the giant bonsai.")

From a corner of Tenju, the voice of a darling little girl could be heard. This was the corner owned by House Masaki, one of the four Houses that formed the Jurai Imperial Family, with Azusa, the current Emperor, as its head.

"Oniisama! Yosho-oniisama!!" A girl energetically leapt through the window of the room of Azusa's son, Masaki Yosho Jurai. She could have been mistaken for a young Sasami, with the light blue-green, spiky hair that was just like her mother's. There were leaves stuck all over her and her clothes.

"Found you!" She pounced with a huge smile at Yosho, who was reading in his study.

"Ayeka, I told you not to come in through the window. Father will yell at you again if he finds out." Yosho spoke harshly, but a wry smile was on his lips, rendering his scolding useless.

Ayeka, in fact, was still smiling. "But Mother Misaki does it, too."

"Good grief…" Yosho sighed, looking at Ayeka's carefree smile. Yes, Jurai's Second Empress, and Ayeka's mother, Misaki, used the exterior of Tenju like her personal highway. Misaki had been doing this since her childhood and hadn't changed even after she became a mother herself. It could have been considered incomparable innocence, but for Yosho, it was exceedingly annoying. Because…

"Yosho-chan! Good *mor*ning!!" Every morning at a certain time, Misaki climbed the outside of Tenju and showed up at Yosho's bedroom window, with her oblivious, gold-star, chirrupy voice. Yosho was twelve already, and it was humiliating to have an older woman call him "Yosho-chan" to wake him up, not to mention see him sleeping. It was for the simple reason that when it came to a man's physiology, Yosho was no exception. However…

"Good morning, Misaki-sama. You seem well today." Yosho

would smile sweetly to greet Misaki, desperately trying to keep his twitching face under control. Otherwise, Misaki would grow morose, sticking her ice-cold hands into his bed to tickle him and rip his comforter off. *Anything but that...*

Yosho discreetly pressed his front, waiting for this tornado to pass. *A tornado would be better... It would never be as often as every morning,* he thought.

"Oniisama. Say, Oniisama. Yosho-oniisama!!"

"What?!" Ayeka's voice brought Yosho back to the present. "I'm sorry, Ayeka. What is it?"

"So, I was listening to Mother and Mother Funaho talking."

"You climbed all the way up there again?" His shock was understakable. The Imperial Palace where Misaki and Funaho lived was almost at the top of Tenju...several hundred meters above Yosho's room. There was a safety net system in place, but the risk was not negligible. "What if you fell? And you shouldn't eavesdrop."

"Yeah, but—"

Yosho pressed his finger to Ayeka's protesting lips and said, "Nobody wants you to get hurt. Utsutsumi-sama, Seto-sama, Father, Mother, and Misaki-sama would be very sad."

"You, too...?" Ayeka asked, with upturned eyes.

"Yes, of course."

"Okay, I won't do it anymore." Cheeks flushed, Ayeka spoke with a tiny voice.

"Good girl."

"Um, so..." Ayeka looked up again, eager to tell him something.

"What is it?"

"Um, they said I'm going to marry you one day. That's what Mother and Mother Funaho were saying."

"What?!" Yosho opened his eyes wide. He had thought about the possibility, but he was surprised at his own reaction now that it was reality. "Is that true?"

"Y-yeah…"

Two weeks later, Yosho and Ayeka's engagement was put on the agenda at the Supreme Council. Yosho was twelve. Ayeka was still four years old.

Masaki Yosho Jurai was born under difficult circumstances. His biological mother, Funaho, came from a planet outside of Jurai (a colonial frontier, even) and yet here she was as First Empress. His father was the Emperor of Jurai, complicating things further. After Funaho claimed the Second Generation Royal Tree Mizuho (Misaki's Tree's name was Karin—the word for cirrocumulus clouds on Jurai—and this Tree was the twin of Mizuho) there was some temporary peace. Although half of the Jurai Imperial Palace felt favorable towards Funaho, the other half was neutral or critical. As far as popularity rates went, things weren't too bad. Hers were among the highest in the history of past Empresses. The problem was that the ones who were critical or neutral were relatively higher in status. Even if she had half of the *total* support, it did not translate to a balance of power. The division of support fell along House lines. House Amaki, Shuzan's clan, was critical. The people who refrained did so out of respect for Utsutsumi from House Kamiki. House Tatsuki remained neutral.

After the First Prince Yosho was born, the criticism abated, but growing up among this silent pressure made him conscious beyond necessity of improving his mother Funaho's standing. Ever since he was little, he worried about Funaho, and whenever he found time, he tried to stay by her side. He believed that it was to protect her physically and psychologically in the place of his father, who was busy with his royal duties. When he named his Tree at the Tree Selection Ceremony after his mother, that was certainly one of the factors.

Yosho underwent the Tree Selection Ceremony when he was eight and had been summoned by the trees, just like Funaho and Misaki. Where he met Funaho the Tree was, strangely enough, the same place where Kirito had been growing when the current Emperor of Jurai, Azusa, formed his contract several decades ago.

Funaho was young and quite small among the stout First Generation Trees. Although she was only as tall as a Second Generation Tree, the energy within her was formidable, and enough to surpass other First Generation Trees.

To have a First Generation Tree was to have absolute power. Nobody on Jurai could defy someone with a First Generation Tree. This was because the Trees' power weakened further down the generations. But in the past several thousand years, now that it was rare for an Imperial Family ship to be engaged in combat, awareness of the generational difference in absolute power had faded. Political power, instead of the power of numbers, was trying to take over, and Amaki Shuzan was at the center of this. That was the world in which Yosho lived.

"Hello, Yosho-dono." Seto, the wife of Utsutsumi and head of family of House Kamiki, respectfully bowed to Yosho, walking down the hallway of Tenju. She was Misaki's biological mother.

"Seto-sama. Hello." Yosho bowed as well, with an expression of relief. Seto was one of Funaho's few allies and someone Yosho and Funaho could depend on. Even the Emperor of Jurai, the most powerful person on the planet, was indebted to her. Now that the previous Emperor had passed, there was nobody on the planet who could speak their mind to her face. Her husband, Utsutsumi, and Emperor Azusa could not express any personal, self-centered opinions (anything that gave them a guilty conscience)...out of fear.

To any malcontent with an ulterior motive, Seto was a terrifying monster. Seto told it like it was, which made her seem boorish, but she was frightfully meticulous and sensitive. For someone of Seto's status, the profound bow she gave Yosho could have been a less formal one, even for a Crown Prince. But she gave him her utmost respect because she knew that others would have to follow her example.

"Is Funaho-sama in?" Seto asked.

"Yes, she's waiting with Misaki-sama in her room."

"Thank you." They exchanged pleasantries, and Seto watched Yosho leave with a smile, then slowly proceeded to Funaho's room.

"Seto-sama, thank you for coming!" Funaho welcomed her with delight. There were no stiff formalities between them as there were with Yosho. Seto treated Funaho just like her daughter, Misaki. This was, in a sense, by design. In a situation that was the reverse of the one with Yosho, this friendliness was a check on the anti-Funaho faction. She was using her own status to protect Funaho, but more than that, she was fond of Funaho's honest and guileless personality. She had realized recently that Funaho was similar in presence to a Royal Tree. Misaki, difficult to handle when she was little, had grown more easygoing because of the sense of security she felt around Funaho.

"About Yosho-dono and Ayeka-chan—I arranged it so that it will be on the agenda for the Supreme Council tomorrow, to get official permission."

"Thank you, Seto-sama."

"My husband has settled down since Ayeka-chan was born, and I think this engagement will be plenty beneficial for Jurai, and... I'm sorry."

"Don't worry about it. I know what our position requires. Yosho will understand. And I think Ayeka-chan will be a very good match for him, too."

"I, too, will have peace of mind with Yosho-dono as her partner..." Seto said, but there was some hesitation in her words.

"Mother, Ayeka-chan is so happy that she'll get to marry Yosho-chan. I love Yosho-chan, too. I've always wanted a little brother." Misaki, left out until now, interrupted with a beaming smile. However, the slightest cloud flashing over Seto's face at

Misaki's words did not escape Funaho's notice. "And then... Oh! It's still a secret."

Funaho looked at the chuckling Misaki and said, "What secret, Misaki-chan?"

"Oh no, I made a promise with Ayeka-chan, Funaho-onee-sama. But you'll find out before their engagement is announced." Misaki smiled, happy that she was able to join the conversation.

"Misaki...stop entering Yosho-dono's room from the exterior." It was abrupt but stated so casually anyone listening would have assumed it was no big deal.

"...!" Funaho realized what Seto had been trying to say.

"What?! But..."

"I'm not criticizing your habit of taking walks outside. But Yosho-dono is twelve now and about to join the ranks of adults. It'll be embarrassing for him if people find out he's called 'Yosho-chan' and has to be woken by you every morning!"

"Urk...but..." Misaki looked up reproachfully. She was married and had a daughter herself, but this kind of thing showed she was still a child.

"But what?" Still with a smile, Seto put pressure on Misaki.

"Urk...b-but..." Normally, Misaki would surrender at this point, but she was a little tenacious today. She slowly made her way towards Funaho to get her on her side (a high-level technique for Misaki), but such a childish tactic would never work on Seto, and they were quickly split apart.

"It's about time you start treating Yosho-dono as an adult."

"All right..." With a frown pursing her lips and large tears spilling over her cheeks, Misaki left the room without a word. By now she was probably yelling insults at her mother, crying, while she climbed up and down Tenju. Today's incident would probably be forgotten after two trips up and down all five thousand meters of Tenju, and she would be back by dinner. Seto saw her off and looked at Funaho with a slight sigh.

"I hadn't realized..." Funaho murmured, her head bowed. It made sense. Yosho was not as fierce as Azusa, but they were very similar. And Misaki took after Seto. It was only natural that Misaki would grow fond of Yosho.

"I'm sorry," Seto said with downcast eyes "My husband and now Misaki, we keep being a nuisance to House Masaki."

"Oh, please don't worry about it. And it's no nuisance... we're family, after all."

This was what Seto loved about Funaho. *She's so cute...* She felt tears welling up in her eyes and hastily added, "Yosho-dono himself hasn't noticed yet. If Misaki doesn't do anything further to draw attention to it..." Seto thought back to the time she met Azusa. His passionate and straightforward gaze. "Yosho-dono is much more mature than Azusa-chan was at that age," she said, almost to herself.

Funaho chuckled, "From your perspective, he's forever 'Azusa-chan,' isn't he?"

"What...?!" Seto's cheeks flushed pink, which was unusual for her. "Good grief, I suppose I'm not one to talk about Misaki." She smiled shyly. When Seto talked about how Azusa was in the past, she became slightly vulnerable. She would normally never let herself blush at someone's words and carelessly reveal her emotions.

Of course, only Funaho, who spent time with her in her private life, could notice these minute reactions.

"Azusa-sama and Yosho have similar temperaments." Funaho wondered if she should ask what she'd known for a while.

Seto smiled mischievously, to answer Funaho. "I sometimes wonder…if Azusa-chan had been born earlier. Next to him would be me…and Mitsuki-dono," she mumbled sadly but wistfully.

Funaho felt no jealousy. She only felt that she would have wanted to see it. "I would imagine that that would make him invincible," she chuckled.

"Yes, but Funaho-dono," Seto slowly cupped Funaho's cheeks with both hands and leaned closer. "You're not as insignificant as you believe. For Azusa-chan…Misaki, and me, you have no idea how much peace you bring just by being here…"

"You, too, Seto-sama? I'm not…"

"I think the way things are now is the way it should be. I have a premonition. Something is going to change, even the fate of Jurai. Your new blood will change something. That's how I feel. And…"

"And?"

"I can't quit being the sarcastic older woman," Seto cackled, blowing away her earlier bashfulness.

"Poor Azusa-sama…"

At that, Seto laughed even louder. Then she winked and said, "Don't tell my husband."

The next morning, the sunlight shone onto Yosho's cheek as he lay in bed, and he sighed. *It's almost time… Oh, here she is.* There was the sound of Misaki coming down the outer wall. Usually, she would fling open the window and come flying into his room, but just before that happened, the rustling of the leaves stopped. Yosho looked quizzically towards the window. He could not see Misaki but heard a hesitant voice.

"Yosho-cha... I mean, Yosho-dono. Are you awake?"

"Yes. Good morning, Misaki-sama."

"I can't wake you up from now on. I'm sorry."

"I can wake up by myself now. Please don't worry about it."

"Yes, you're grown up now... See you later, Yosho-dono." The rustling sound grew further and further away. Misaki would never have come to this conclusion on her own. And she used the -dono suffix instead of -chan. Yosho understood that Seto must have said something to her.

He let out a small sigh as he heard the distant rustling. He did not notice that it was not a sigh of relief. He did not realize his own feelings. At twelve years old, he was growing up, but also still a child.

What allowed him to realize it was what happened that night. The doorbell rang.

"Who is it?"

Ayeka's tentative voice was heard from the other side. "Oniisama..."

"Ayeka? You never come through the front entrance. Come in." Normally, Ayeka would enter with a big smile. But noticing that she was not coming in, Yosho closed the book he was reading and stood up. "What's the matter? You're so quiet today... Hm?!"

He opened the door, saw Ayeka standing there, and caught his breath.

It was indeed Ayeka, but her hair was a dark purple, and the spiky hair was beautifully coiffed. "Ayeka… Your hair…" The only pictures Yosho had seen of Funaho were when she was past age fourteen. But he was sure that, when she was young, she must have looked like Ayeka did now. That thought made him realize that Ayeka, wanting to become Yosho's ideal woman, had edited her genes to match her father, who had similar hair to Funaho. *It's true I thought of my mother as the ideal woman. But…*

"Yosho-oniisama. Does my hair…look weird?" Ayeka asked nervously, but with childlike, determined eyes.

"What did Misaki-sama say…?"

"She said I looked cute. She held me tight and wouldn't let go for an hour."

"I see. It looks good on you, Ayeka…" Belying his words, he felt a stabbing pain in his heart. He finally realized that it had started when Ayeka spoke of the engagement, though he still did not understand why. Yosho did not dislike Ayeka. He was keenly aware of his mother's position. But what brother would resent a little sister with such sincere feelings towards him? However, the pain continued. It throbbed intensely inside him. He was desperate that it not be noticed, so he laughed, and said, "It looks really good on you."

"Thank you, Oniisama. I'll go show everyone!"

"Okay…"

She nodded, satisfied and happy that her favorite brother complimented her, and ran down the hallway. Her retreating figure, innocently skipping down the hall, overlapped with an image of Misaki, as parent and child might.

Yosho's expression clouded. He recognized what the feelings within him were.

The next morning, he woke up at the usual time, and heard the rustling of leaves from Misaki climbing down from afar. He imagined her face smiling with glee as she thought about surprising him in his sleep. Yosho's heart beat faster. The rustling stopped near his room. Misaki would normally shout, laughing, "Yosho-chan, good *mor*ning!!" The tension Yosho felt inside peaked. Yes, that was how it usually went... However...

"Good morning, Yosho-dono..." Misaki spoke through the wall, hidden from view. It was not her usual cheerful tone. She sounded in a little bit of a funk, like the day before.

"Good morning, Misaki-sama," Yosho answered with as much calm as he could muster so Misaki would not notice. He sat up and held himself back from rushing to the window.

Without another word, Misaki started moving again. Yosho felt a sting in his eyes. The tears that eventually fell from the corners of his eyes stained his pillow a slightly darker color. He mumbled, his lips trembling. "Misaki...sama..." He remained still on his bed until he could no longer hear the rustling. That was his new morning routine.

A few days later, Seto came to visit Yosho's room. Seto hardly ever came to see him in his room. "Seto-sama, I would have gone to see you if there were a matter to attend to."

"Funaho-dono gifted some fruit to me. I couldn't wait until I got home to eat them, so I thought about having tea here. I wanted to talk to you, too." Having given this spiel, Seto entered without waiting for Yosho's reply.

She's as aggressive as always when it comes to tea... Yosho, with a wry smile, invited Seto in.

The fruit Seto brought were persimmons. Funaho had given Azusa some as souvenirs as he was about to leave Earth; they had kept the seeds and planted them here. Seto took a sip of the tea Yosho served and began to talk.

"What?! Me, the Galaxy Academy?"

"Yes. You know how we send about ten students every year in a goodwill exchange program."

"Yes. So I should go next year?"

"No, *this* year."

"But I thought they already left, last month."

"There's no hard and fast rule. I'm not saying you have to; it's a voluntary program..." Seto turned with a meaningful look.

Why is she bringing this up all of a sudden...? Yosho was confused, not knowing Seto's true intent. Many Galaxy Academy graduates took important posts in countries throughout the galaxy. Yosho knew it was a good opportunity for him to expand his future network of contacts. Seto probably thought it was faster for Yosho to strengthen his own foundations abroad, to become accepted as Crown Prince on Jurai, than staying with the Emperor, who still stood on shaky political ground. But going to study abroad the very next month seemed rather hasty. And this was after this year's students had already been sent.

Yosho cast his eyes downward and mulled things over in his mind; without discerning an acceptable answer, he once again turned to Seto. Seto looked displeased, but it was not about Yosho. It was something else.

Oh...! Seto was looking not at Yosho but the last piece of persimmon. Yosho had not eaten even a single piece yet. That meant Seto had eaten all the fruit she had brought herself. She could not bring herself to take the last piece, but she could not bear to have that last piece taken from her. That was why she was in a bad mood.

She's definitely Misaki-sama's mother...! Suddenly, he realized why she suggested studying abroad. Seto was giving him the chance to put some distance between himself and Misaki. Yosho was grateful to her and offered her the last persimmon.

"Seto-sama...I'll take the study abroad. Thank you for considering me."

"Oh, are you sure?"

"Please." He watched Seto happily eat the fruit and felt freedom and loss at the same time. What did the persimmon taste like? Yosho mulled over these things in his mind.

Once Yosho decided to study at Galaxy Academy, he had his days full since the time until departure was so soon. The Supreme Council decided that Yosho and Ayeka's engagement would take place in two years, after the period of study was over. They also decided that it was too early to make an announcement and only announced his plans of study to other countries.

"O-Oniisama. I'll always be waiting for you." Until Yoshi's departure, Ayeka visited his room often, repeated these words like an incantation, and burst into tears. Yosho was at a loss when Misaki, who had also anxiously come to see how things were going, also burst into tears. He promised them he would come home twice a year.

"Good luck with your studies," Funaho said on the night before departure. She also meant, "Find closure for your feelings toward Misaki."

"I set out tomorrow," Yosho mumbled to himself as he crawled into bed. The next day would be the end of his morning routine. He looked forward to hearing the rustling of leaves and quietly closed his eyes.

Yosho

Yosho's royal ship had the same name as his mother: Funaho. Sailing at full speed through space, her bridge showed a star system on its main monitor. It was Galaxy Academy, a giant educational institution that utilized an entire star system in a neutral zone near the boundaries of Jurai. It used to be a Juraian Royal facility, but 20,000 years ago, it transferred to the Galactic Federation. At the time of its founding, there were six natural planets and one artificial planet, but four additional artificial planets were added since. With several thousand satellites bigger than colonies, and more construction as large as space stations being built daily, making an accurate estimate of its size was impossible.

It was a treasure trove of knowledge, an institution that fundamentally supported the prosperity of humanity, and also a kind of Pandora's Box.

The bridge's main monitor switched to the central and biggest planet in the Academy. There was neither bodyguard nor a single servant accompanying him. Even Yosho was nervous, though there was nobody who could harm the Jurai Royal Family after bio-augmentation. It was the center of scientific research in the galaxy, but the Academy's security department had a good reputation, so the likelihood of anything happening was low. Most of all, Yosho was aboard the First Generation battleship Funaho, the best in the fleet even among the most powerful Jurai ships. Taking along security guards on top of this would be shameful. And taking along servants would be like your mother coming along to a boarding school. Yosho was twelve already, and he knew he had to be able to do things for himself.

"We're almost there," Yosho mumbled to nobody in particular, turned Funaho's course to the space port on the central planet, and prepared to dock.

Nobody was there to greet him when he disembarked. He did not expect a glorious reception, but he did feel a shock at the gap between this and what he had been used to on Jurai.

So that's what my existence amounts to in the world outside... In this situation, it really sank in that he had left his home world behind. Relieved from having to attend ceremonies and his royal duties, he felt lighter.

"Welcome to the Galaxy Academy, Masaki Yosho Jurai-kun." A girl, presumably a student, spoke to Yosho from behind. She continued, as if she read his thoughts through his expression. "Are you surprised? A Juraian Crown Prince should get a bigger welcome... Am I right, Yosho-kun?"

At the Academy, a volunteer student guide was assigned to someone who entered partway through the academic year. She was supposed to look after him through the process. The girl, three years his senior, introduced herself, hand outstretched. "My name is Airi Magma. Nice to meet you."

"I'm Masaki Yosho Jurai... Magma-dono, what you meant earlier..."

"Magma-*dono*?!" Airi exclaimed with a grimace.

"Did I offend you? On Jurai, this is the normal way to address people."

"Oh no, that's not what I meant. I just wasn't used to that... Just call me Airi." She laughed, a little embarrassed.

"All right, Airi-dono."

"So...I just said... Oh well, you'll need some adjusting." She gave a hidden sigh. He was the Jurai Crown Prince, after all.

"Um, Airi-dono?"

"Sorry I interrupted... Were you surprised at the cold welcome? The son of the most powerful person in the biggest country in the galaxy has come here, but there's no pomp and circumstance. Only a single female student to welcome him." It sounded sarcastic, but Airi did not mean it that way. She was honestly expressing herself, thought Yosho. Her blunt personality was refreshing to him.

He answered honestly, "Yes, I realized that my existence is much smaller off Jurai."

"Are you really only twelve...?" His reaction was unexpected for Airi. A twelve-year-old boy being so naturally mature was a surprise. She furrowed her brows and leaned closer to observe such a curiosity.

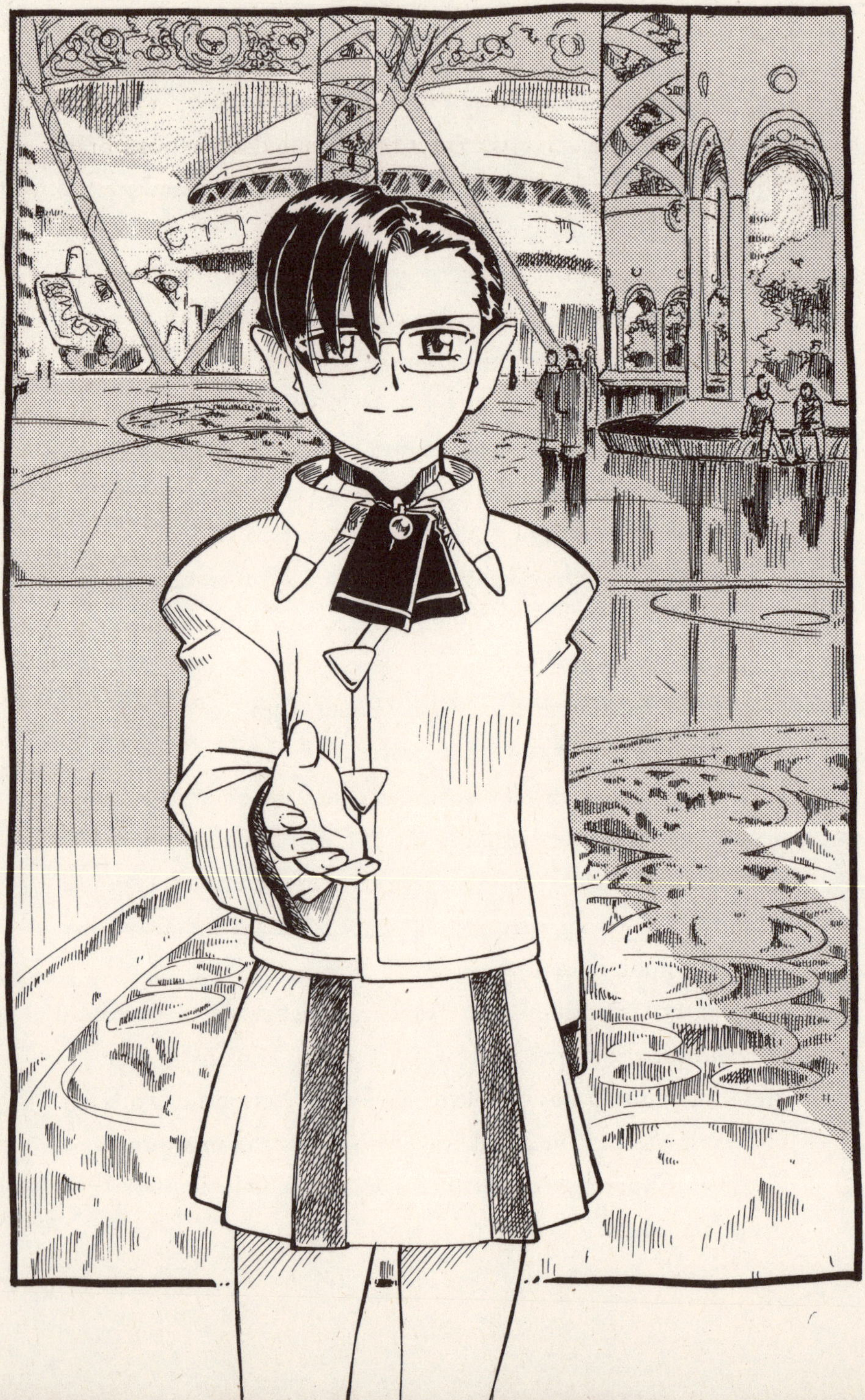

"Yes...I am..."

"How boring... I was expecting a spoiled obnoxious brat throwing a tantrum that things had to be exactly his way."

"Huh?"

"There are a lot of guys like that, especially the special transfer students. Most of it is the parents' fault... They think this is a tourist destination or something. The guy who came before you, the relative of a Jurai Royal, came on a flashy Royal Ship, with a crowd of attendants... Even though the power he had in his country meant nothing here," Airi spat out with contempt, and Yosho nodded in agreement. "Looks like you're all right, but you should be careful. Trouble resulting from quarrels between countries is taken to the Judicial Administration, and worst case, the parties involved can be expelled. You didn't come on a Royal Ship? Your ship looks like a small cruiser," said Airi, looking at Yosho's ship moored in port.

No wonder. Funaho was camouflaged with a metal hull. The Royal Tree core unit was not very big to begin with, and with the hull units removed, only as big as a small cruiser. However, what lay inside was more powerful and destructive than an entire country's military. An extraordinary monster.

"No, I didn't bring her this time." The existence of the Royal Trees inside the Royal Ships was top secret, and anyone not in the Royal Family was unable to see inside. No matter the facts, or how it was explained, a Royal Ship in international space was considered a battleship under galactic law. Yosho lied to save himself some trouble.

It was not just Airi. Only a few even among the Royal Family were aware that Yosho had gone to the Academy on Funaho, and a dummy unit was attached to Funaho's outer hull units, which were left on the planet Jurai. There was no need to do this with Second or Third Generation Trees, but Yosho was on a First Generation ship, of which only four existed in the entire history of Jurai, so of course Jurai was being careful.

"Oh...you don't seem to have brought an entourage either. Different strokes for different folks, even among the Jurai Royal Family, I guess. But I'm a bit disappointed."

"About what...?"

"I was looking forward to straightening out the rich idiot using his power as a shield." Airi clenched her fists and looked up at the sky. She probably was planning to literally straighten him with those fists.

Seeing her, Yosho chuckled internally. *I thought I felt an odd affinity... She's a little bit like Seto-sama. I wonder if my fate binds me to these types of people.* He looked over at Airi, who was peering into Yosho's face. "What is it?"

"Maybe it's still the same thing in a different way..." Airi mumbled to herself.

A chill went up Yosho's spine. "What do you mean?"

"Nothing. Oh, I'll tell you one thing. Like you said, your existence means nothing here."

He may have thought it, but being told outright by someone else made even Yosho feel depressed.

Airi chuckled, then pointing at Yosho, said gently but

forcefully, "But it's an opportunity. What you create here will be undoubtedly all your own. The reputation you earn here will spread far and wide."

"My own...?"

"Yes! So work hard... And there's going to be a welcome party for you tonight. It's just a private, informal thing."

"Thank you." Walking behind Airi, he felt a lump in his throat. *What you create here will be undoubtedly all your own...* These words might have been what Yosho had wanted the most. What could he establish here? Coming to Galaxy Academy, what Yosho obtained first was the possibility called Freedom.

That night...

"Airi-dono...how is this private and informal?" Yosho shouted at Airi even though she was right next to him. The town was teeming with crowds of people as far as the eye could see. It was like a festival or parade of the entire Academy, completely the reverse of the tranquility during the day.

Airi winked at Yosho as he blinked in astonishment. "Ha ha, surprised? But this isn't just for you."

"What do you mean?"

"People from all over the galaxy come here, from a variety of backgrounds, religions, and faiths. They all have special holidays. Birthdays, too. You want people to celebrate them, and you *want* to celebrate for them. That's why there's some kind of celebration every day. It would be a pain to celebrate each and every one of them, so we do them all together."

"Does that mean…there's a party like this *every* day?"

"Not every day. Every *night*. You gotta study during the day, that's what students are here for. Here, put this on." She shoved a hat with a large mark on Yosho.

"What is this?"

"Don't take it off. It's to mark you."

"Mark?" He looked around to see others with the same things on their heads. At the same time, someone slapped him on the back, and Yosho saw a man he had never met before smiling at him.

"Congratulations."

"Th-thank you?" Yosho stared blankly as the man walked off again, and many more came to talk to him. It seemed to be that anyone wearing these hats was someone celebrating something that day.

"Congratulations."

"Thank you." As the night wore on, their excited welcomes got more flamboyant. A woman with bright lipstick and a form-fitting dress clung to him, drunk. "Oh, he's so cute! Come on, won't you let me be your guide? I can take you places. You know what I mean!"

"Well, that's…" Yosho was flustered in spite of himself.

"Oh, how precious!"

"I'm afraid he's too young for the places you can take him." Airi wedged herself between them.

"Oh, you're his guide, Airi? Oh, poor thing," she chuckled.

"What do you…"

"Later." The woman disappeared into the crowd without answering his question. The congratulations were incessant, but their curiosity seemed focused on seeing the student for whom Airi had chosen to be a guide.

Airi-dono seems to be famous, Yosho understood from the snippets of conversations.

"You're the foreign student. Congratulations. What's your name?"

"Masaki Yosho Jurai." As soon as Yosho answered with his full name to the women who surrounded him, the place instantly fell silent.

"Yes, he's the Crown Prince of Jurai." Airi smiled, and the original party mood gradually returned.

Why did everyone fall silent at mention of Jurai? When he tried to ask Airi, another onslaught of shrill (female) voices squealed. Older women tended to flock to him. Alcohol-fueled, the women hugged him and showered his cheeks with kisses. Without even needing to inhale the scent of perfume and alcohol, Yosho was drunk on their soft cheeks and bosoms.

Boom. Boom. Fireworks lit up the sky.

"Is it that time already? Well, good night." Everyone around him bid him good night one by one and left. The fireworks were the signal for curfew for those in junior high and below.

"Yosho-kun, let's go."

"Oh, right. Thank you for today," Yosho bowed to the people waving. Reluctant to part, several women surrounded him and would not let go. Airi practically snatched him away.

"You're so popular, Yosho-kun." Airi gave a sidelong glance. She was clearly having fun with this.

"That's not true."

"Oh yeah?" The two of them walked on, pushed by the flow of the crowd, but that crowd dwindled in the side streets. The night breeze felt good on their tired bodies. Airi stopped and turned in front of the junior high dorm. "I've registered you for your room already, so just do what they say. Good night."

Yosho hastily stopped her from walking off, "Airi-dono! I'll walk you to your dorm."

"Mine? But you're younger than me..." She paused. "Well, thanks. But there's some place I have to go. I have a few more friends who are celebrating tonight. Good night." She winked at him and ran towards the crowd.

"Oh..." Yosho stared at her receding form and felt he had missed his chance to ask why everyone reacted strangely when he stated his full name. *I'll casually ask when I see her tomorrow,* he thought and cut through the dorm courtyard towards his room. Just then...

Someone's there...! He felt someone watching him. It was obvious to Yosho, since their ability to mask their presence was still immature—by the standards of Juraians, who had unparalleled combat skills. Judging by another star system's standards, they were good enough to be professionals.

Yosho pretended to be distracted by something to create an opening, and five shadows leapt towards him. They'd been tricked.

They're Juraian. Their self-carriage and combat style confirmed it for Yosho. The battle among obstacles using the trees in the courtyard was the specialty of Jurai martial arts, and the movement of the shadows were naive but demonstrated its basics rules of combat. Because of that, Yosho could read their moves. The battle was over all too easily, not even befitting the description of combat.

Around Yosho were scattered five groaning boys. They were the ones who had attacked him. It was not by random chance that a twelve year old could easily defeat five boys. Yosho had talented masters who trained him—the Emperor of Jurai, Misaki, Seto, Utsutsumi—who were exceptional even among the Royal Family. Misaki treated Yosho as her little brother, so she kept harassing him whenever she could. With Yosho being used to Misaki's speed, the fastest on Jurai, ordinary Juraian children did not stand a chance, even if they were older.

Did I go too far...? Yosho tried to check on the boys, then stopped. It would be humiliating for Juraian men to have their opponent show them concern. And there was another reason.

"Did you also have business with me?" he said to the dark bushes. He had noticed that another group had been watching him. He knew from their ability to mask their presence that they were more skilled than the previous boys, but it was not much of a difference to Yosho. The leader made a signal, and the others carried away the boys Yosho had defeated. The only ones remaining in the courtyard were the leader and Yosho.

"My name is Hirata Kanemitsu." He looked fearless and was strongly built, but his large eyes were endearing. Those eyes made an impression on Yosho.

"I'm Masaki Yosho Jurai." Yosho also introduced himself, but it was not to fight. There was no hostile aura between them.

"Your status or power on Jurai means nothing here. Anyone who relies on them will be ridiculed. Even so, there are great fools who sometimes don't get it. They're usually royals and their families." Kanemitsu looked down at the spot on the grass where the boys had been. "The guys who attacked you were sent by those idiots."

"What do you want with me?"

"I came to warn you. Your power will be useless, but it doesn't erase the fact that you're a Juraian Royal, and sometimes that may actually cause problems instead. The Amaki idiot brought a whole entourage and became a laughingstock."

"I'll keep that in mind..."

"There are other things... Hm?!" The bell to signal lights out tolled just then. They had to be in their rooms before the dorm monitors started their rounds. "Get a different guide."

"Are you talking about Airi-dono?"

"Who's there?" A dorm monitor heard their voices and swung his flashlight around.

"Do your own research. Later."

"I appreciate the warning."

The flashlight beam lit up where they had been standing. "It's past lights out! You better..." The angry monitor widened his eyes in surprise. The students were nowhere to be seen.

Back in his own room, Yosho took a shower to wash off the sweat and mulled over what Kanemitsu had said. "Replace Airi-dono... The only thing I can think of is everyone's reaction at the celebration upon hearing I'm from Jurai. That must be related." He exited the bathroom and changed into his night clothes, toweled dry his hair, and pressed the home button on the access device he brought.

"Funaho, please check the Academy personnel data banks. Give me the profile on my guide, Airi Magma-dono."

In a few seconds, the terminal displayed the information. "From the planetary nation Airai... Head temple of Airain. Daughter of its leader, Gaira Magma! So that's what it was..."

With that information, all his questions were resolved. Airain was the largest religious group in the galaxy, spreading its influence everywhere, and its members surpassing that of the largest nation's population. Ten thousand years ago, it was only the religion of a single country, but a certain discovery increased its popularity explosively.

It began with the fact that a common relic existed on many planets in the galaxy. Visitors from an unknown world, or worlds, made these religious relics. From these relics, primitive religions were derived by the indigenous humanoids or by peoples who came to be after the relics were created.

The establishment of the Galactic Federation enabled communications between different worlds, and concurrently the scientists at the Academy deduced that the relics on each planet had common elements. The mystery that remained was which was the planet of origin for the relics, the true ancestor of the religion? Obviously, many planets tried to claim this title for themselves. The dispute intensified, even leading to wars.

A thousand years later, the Galaxy Academy research team led by Washu discovered its true roots. That was Airai. The fact that religions created by the relics were derived from Airain massively widened its influence.

Here was the problem for Yosho. The major superpowers almost always had an Airain church. Jurai also had freedom of religion, and since it had a history as an aggregate of many people, there was a variety of religious faiths. But currently, aside from a few lingering customs, those religions were no more. Including Airain.

There were churches for those who came to Jurai from abroad, but there were no Juraian believers. There were several reasons for this: one was that most of Jurai's territory was composed of colonies, so no religions with a relic as an idol had emerged. The other was that Jurai itself was in the frontiers of the galaxy, quite distant from Airai, and a relic was not present at all.

The most important reason was that Jurai already had a clear object of worship, and that was the Royal Trees, with Tsunami as progenitor. Airai's belief in its god and Jurai's existing gods couldn't coexist; the people of Jurai did not accept other gods.

It should be noted that "god" here meant something different from the concept of gods of the people of Earth where Tenchi lived. The existence of god had been identified as the awe of Nature, aliens with the technology of interstellar flight, dimensional beings, and intelligent life-forms on a higher plane of existence. In that sense, it differed from the indeterminate gods of primitive beings. In particular, intelligent life-forms on a higher plane of existence possessed overwhelming power even in this technologically advanced age and were often referred to as gods.

Since the creation of Jurai, worship transferred from various idols to the Royal Trees over a period of hundreds of thousands of years.

Of course the people of Airai were hostile to Jurai, considering them heathens. Recently, hard-liners forbade the Royal Ships from their territorial space, and some on Jurai also felt they should retaliate.

Kanemitsu-dono probably feared that I would be taken in by Airai. Ridiculous. Airi-dono isn't devious like that. For better or for worse, Yosho was born into complicated circumstances, and he was sensitive toward people's malice. Yosho was confident that Airi had no ulterior motives. But even if there were no intent, others might not agree. For some, it was a problem that Airi was even in the same place as Yosho. *I must at least prevent Jurai's intervention with respect to Airi-dono...*

Yosho had the ability to accept reality and the means to cope. He had one question. Why did Airi-dono accept being his guide? While he pondered this, he fell asleep.

The next day...

"It's morning..." He waited for the rustling of leaves in bed, as usual. "This is the Galaxy Academy... She's not coming here." Being in a different place did not mean he could simply put that part of his life behind him. He kept waiting for Misaki, who was not coming. "At least until the usual time..." Just then!

"Yosho-kun!!" A loud voice that could wake the dead assaulted Yosho's ears. "Say, Yosho-kun!!"

Yosho's sentiments and his priceless slumber were blown away, sending him tumbling underneath his bed... "A-Airi-dono?!"

Airi's voice came from the communications monitor. "Hey, were you awake?" She laughed on the other side, weirdly chipper for so early in the morning.

"Good morning...Airi-dono."

"What are you wearing?"

"Huh?" He finally realized that he was still in his sleep clothes. "E-excuse me."

"Get changed and come on out. A lot of other transfer students are coming today, so it's going to get crowded if you're late! I'll be waiting at the park across the street." She stated her business and hung up.

Yosho hastily got ready and headed to the park. "I'm sorry I kept you waiting. Good morning."

"Good morning. That didn't take long. I'm impressed!" Airi nodded in satisfaction, her arms crossed. "Let's get the paperwork over with and get breakfast... Oh, but first." She lowered her arms, straightened up and stared at Yosho, and brought up the topic of the questions from last night.

"Say, Yosho-kun...are you sure you want me to continue as your guide?" She was asking because she was certain that he had found out about her yesterday.

Finding this very prudent, Yosho answered cheerfully, "Yes, as long as it's no trouble for you."

"I keep asking, but...are you *sure* you're twelve?" Airi continued, smiling wryly at Yosho. "It might get complicated. I know things are hard for your mother."

"My mother has many people looking out for her, including my father."

"This is about your future, too."

"I believe it's a good thing for Jurai's future for me to have good relations with other countries." There was no falsehood in his words. Airi knew this from looking into his eyes.

"Yosho-kun... No, never mind. Thank you." She saw the sincerity in his eyes, almost commented on it, and suppressed it.

Noticing that, Yosho bowed deeply. "Thank you for your assistance."

"Then that's the end of this topic! I don't want to hear any take backs. If you do, I'll punch your face and curse and hold you in contempt forever." Airi smiled sweetly, talking fast.

She does remind me of Misaki-sama and Seto-sama. Yosho thought briefly that he might have been too hasty, but looking at Airi's happy face, promptly forgot the whole feeling.

A few hours later, the paperwork taken care of and breakfast eaten, Yosho left Airi and returned to his room without asking about what her thoughts had been. He could inquire into that later. There was something more pressing for him. It was the omnipresent feeling that something was out of place ever since he met her. Something was always watching him. It had only been two days, and things had been hectic. Though it certainly might begin and end with his being Jurai Crown Prince.

If it's not my imagination, these are highly trained people, perhaps from a governmental intelligence agency. The problem is... Who were they affiliated with? Any reputable information bureau would already be aware that Yosho was enrolled in the Galaxy Academy.

Well, this might be a nuisance for Airi-dono, but I'll ask her.

He could have called her from Funaho's access device, but he made the call through the terminal supplied in the room to make it easier for others to listen in. After several rings, the display showed the connection. "Airi-dono? Forgive me for calling, but it's Yosho."

"Oh, Yosho-kun... It's so late, what's up?" When she discovered it was Yosho, the audio switched to video.

"I-I'm sorry, I didn't realize you'd already turned in. I'll call back tomorrow..." Dismayed, he spoke quickly. On the monitor was Airi, dressed casually in just a T-shirt. Her hair was disheveled, and though still immature, the shadows of her shirt followed the soft curve of her breasts... All of it quickened Yosho's pulse.

"It's okay. I always dress like this at home. So what's up? Is there something you don't understand?" Airi did not seem to mind Yosho seeing her slovenly outfit. She said she always dressed like this, but she would never have let it be seen on video if it were not Yosho. He was probably more like a little brother to her.

Even so, Yosho, who had never seen a lady dressed like this before, was stunned. His attendants and ladies-in-waiting helped him dress, so he was used to showing others his skin, but he was not used to *seeing* skin. He desperately tried to hide how upset he was and continued, "Well, actually, there's someplace I would like you to go with me..." With blood rushing to his cheeks, he spoke quickly, and Airi chuckled.

"All right... Since you asked, I'll go with you." With how embarrassed he was, she must have thought that he was asking her for a date. But her tone was that of a kindergarten teacher dealing with her ward.

"O-okay, thank you." He hastily specified the time and place, and hung up. He ruminated over her parting words that she was looking forward to it. *I already feel tired even before we've gone out...*

He felt mentally drained and sighed deeply. Now he wondered if it really had to be Airi, but since it was only his second day there, he did not know anyone else. He concluded that his selection was obvious.

I feel like I'm making excuses.

Not true. The voices inside his head sounded like he was trying to persuade himself.

"Oh well," he mumbled to convince himself and reached for Funaho's access device. The Master Key smoothly coordinated with the Royal Tree, and without words, his will reached Funaho. Satisfied, Yosho nodded and spoke gently, "I'm counting on you, Funaho..."

Airi

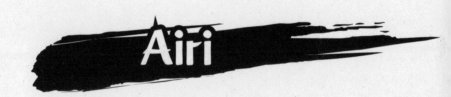

G IRLS GROW FASTER than boys in their early teens. Yosho was twelve and Airi fifteen. At first glance, they seemed more like older sister and younger brother.

"Let's go!" Using Yosho's "date itinerary" as reference (that was the excuse), Airi blazed through like she was checking the items off of a homework assignment.

For Yosho, this "date" had a purpose, and that was to flush out whoever was keeping watch on Yosho and Airi by luring them out under various conceivable conditions. Funaho observed from above, watching an area dozens of kilometers wide for mechanical movements, suspicious people in the crowd, and all kinds of elements to deduce likely suspects. Since he did not know how many they could be, and with the ambiguity of the situation, he had figured it would be impossible to go over the entire itinerary in a single day. He had planned to split it up over a few days. This was the first day...however...

"Let's see, what's next... Oh, let's go over there! Come on!"

Airi took Yosho's hand with excitement in her voice. At this rate, they would complete the itinerary in a single day. There was no chance of sussing anyone out.

"A-Airi-dono, a little more slowly... We don't need to rush so much."

"Come on, get going. Or we won't be able to go through this in one day."

"We don't *have* to do this in one day," Yosho tried to explain but could not contain her momentum.

"Next! Next!" As Airi continued the forced march, Yosho had to wonder if she was doing this on purpose, but her beaming smile was enough to sweep such concerns under the rug. And the more dazzling it was, the more Yosho felt tormented by guilt.

In the end, they completed the route before evening. Airi collapsed, panting and dripping with sweat, on the grass in the park where they had met up that morning. She tried to catch her breath without even bothering to mop her brow.

"Airi-dono, are you all right?" Yosho fanned her with the folding fan he carried.

"Y-Yosho-kun...you look well..." Choking on her words and dragging herself upright, she glared at him with chagrin.

"You should continue to rest..."

"It's too hot...!" She crawled into the shade. "Fan me!" Airi rolled over again and ordered Yosho with a sharp glance.

"Sure."

"You think I'm old...don't you?" Airi mumbled in the dappled light, fanned by Yosho.

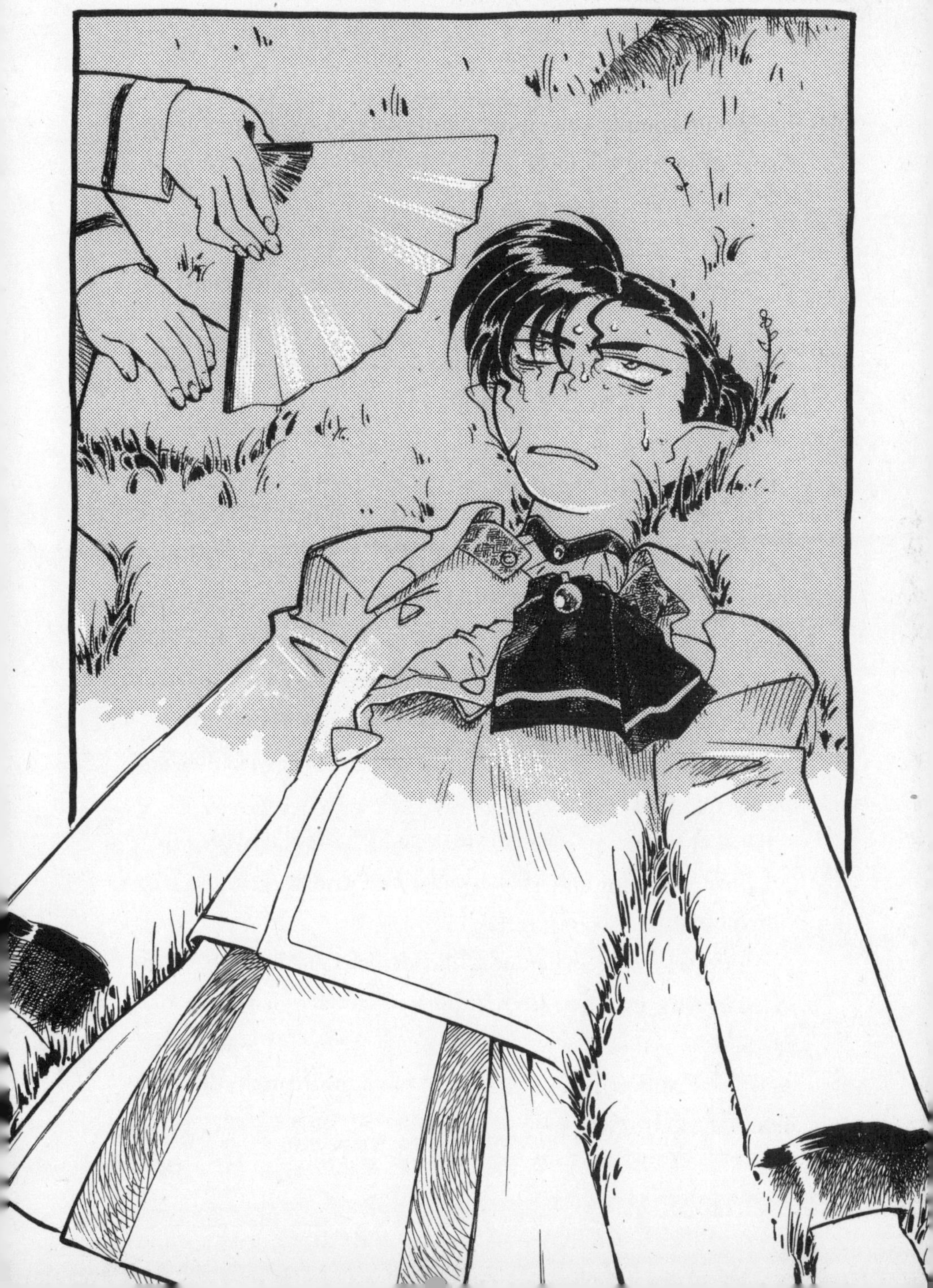

"Huh...?"

"I'm three years and four months older than you. I'm sure you think of me as an old lady." She seemed angry and began to pout.

"I didn't say that."

"But you're thinking it."

"I'm not," Yosho said as calmly and gently as he could. He knew people like her would fixate on an idea, and poke at it until they were satisfied. He had no choice but to take her seriously and be patient. "You ran a lot, so it's only natural."

"Then what about *you*? You're not even out of breath."

"I've been trained."

At those words, all the anger vanished from Airi's eyes. She stared at him in silence. "You should be at least a resentful little... Wipe that enlightenment off your face. You idiot," Airi lightly pinched Yosho's cheek and smiled sadly. She was painfully aware of what kind of world he lived in at the tender age of twelve, and she found his maturity to be pitiable. "Poor Yosho-kun."

Yosho could not respond and let Airi do as she pleased. He did not consider himself pitiable. He was the Crown Prince of Jurai, after all. It was true that there was a lot of friction surrounding his mother, and he felt he wanted to protect her. Was that pitiable?

Airi watched Yosho ponder all this, leapt up, and out of the blue, bonked him on his head. "For the love of... Just laugh!! Cry!!" She screamed and tickled him all over. "Get angry!! You brat!!" She immediately put him into a Cobra Twist-like submission hold. Her words did not correspond to each action.

The passersby simply watched calmly and said, "Oh, she's at it again."

"Poor guy. Who's the new victim?"

"Airi sure is boisterous."

Yosho heard all these snippets of conversation. To the people who lived here, this kind of thing must be a regular occurrence.

"If you're twelve, act like it and show some emotion!!" She put him in something like a Boston Crab this time. She was definitely not going easy on him.

"A-Airi-dono. Everyone's watching... This isn't proper..." Yosho muttered, wincing in pain. If he flexed just a little, he could bounce her off without hurting her, but he understood vaguely how she was feeling and so kept taking the abuse.

"You could at least complain that it hurts..." Airi puffed out her cheeks in frustration and sat down a little ways away.

"I can't do that in public."

"I see... So anyway, why are you doing *that*?" Airi pointed at Yosho's legs. He was sitting formally, with his legs under him and back straight.

"In these situations, I would need permission from the eldest present to be at ease."

Airi bolted upright, straightened the hem of her skirt, and corrected her posture. "Sometimes I wonder if I'm the one with no manners when I'm with you..."

"Huh? What was that? I didn't hear you, could you repeat that?"

"Nothing!"

"Okay..."

"Yeah..." Airi breathed a sigh of relief. Yosho didn't press further. The conversation abruptly broke off into an awkward silence. In that silence, the bell tolling five o'clock echoed from the distance. Airi took this opportunity and said with obvious relief, "S-say...shall we have dinner, if you don't have plans after this?"

"Well, there's the restaurant we passed."

"Go to expensive places like that when you want to show off to your actual girlfriend. I know a good place near here." Airi felt much better after resting and pulled Yosho along in much the same way as before.

"A-Airi-dono, we don't have to hurry." The more Yosho pleaded, the more Airi rushed. They ended up running, threading through the throngs of people.

The place Airi took them, a restaurant called Narsis, was on the second floor of a large mall next to the park. It did not look distinctive but more like a garden-variety run-of-the-mill restaurant. But when she brought him to the terrace, Yosho opened his eyes wide at the majestic view.

"Wh-what is this place?!" In front of them was a seven-hundred-meter cliff carved by a giant cylinder about a dozen kilometers wide. Beyond that, the ocean spread before them. Yosho hastily confirmed where they were on the guide map, but such a place was not listed. Only a red square denoting "secret" obliterated the spot. Important research facilities were often not made public. It was optically processed to be camouflaged from above.

"Surprised? Isn't this an amazing view?" Airi, seeing his shock, was delighted.

"But isn't this a restricted area?"

"How could there be a mall in a restricted area? That map means 'don't tell anyone.'"

"Tell...?"

"Don't you get it?" She chuckled. "This place is hidden to surprise the people who come here for the first time." Airi was cheerful, having worked through her earlier dissatisfaction.

"To surprise people? That's the only reason...?"

"Yes, that's it. It's just a prank."

"Isn't this too elaborate?"

Airi laughed then said with a straight face, "Yosho-kun, that's exactly the kind of place Galaxy Academy is." The expression correctly captured the Academy's true essence. "It's to surprise people who come to the Academy for the first time. They put in a few places like this, and the students add their own twists. They can have a simple reveal or an ambitious prank..."

According to Airi, this was a crater fifty kilometers wide created by an accident of an experimental device gone awry, and who should have made it, but none other than Professor Washu? It should have been fixed right away, but the students who Washu had been toying with...or rather, was doting on, waged a massive campaign to preserve a rare example of Washu having made a mistake.

"Hmph! This is nothing but a pore," commented Washu; and with that, this attraction was christened "Washu's Pore." This horrible taste in names was characteristic of Academy students.

Looking out the window at the landscape, Airi murmured,

"Yosho-kun, the area around the crater is the facilities for the philosophy department."

"Philosophy?!" It was no small wonder he was surprised. The philosophy department consolidated the wealth of knowledge from all fields, unifying it into one theory, and decided policies based on ethics. The philosophy department was where the greatest minds of Galaxy Academy gathered. "Then this size makes sense."

"This is only part of it, and the facilities are for a single department member."

"One person is using this whole place?"

"It's not a rarity for philosophy, but this is special. It's a sort of memorial hall, too."

"A memorial hall?"

"You might've heard of Hakubi Washu and Akara Naja, the best of the Academy and legendary philosophers. This is their hall of achievements."

"I know of Hakubi Washu but not Akara Naja…"

"Naja had more of a supportive role. If you're interested, I can show you around. That place is like my backyard… Although the philosopher there right now is an old man, and he'll tell you tales of the good old days over tea for hours." Airi bore the distinctive smile of one who had experienced this firsthand.

Yosho was momentarily captivated by her expression, when in front of him were placed some delicious-smelling dishes. "Welcome, Airi. This must be the person from Jurai you were talking about. It took a whole month for you to bring him here? That's not like you." The middle-aged waitress laughed.

"No, this is the next guy."

"My name is Masaki Yosho Jurai. Nice to meet you," Yosho assessed that she was Airi's acquaintance and stood to introduce himself.

"Well, well, what a polite fellow. My name is Karsa Igulier. I own this place. In any case, the Jurai in your name means..."

"He's the Crown Prince of Jurai."

"So this must be his third day here. Wow..." She stared at Yosho, impressed, but placed the dishes deftly on the table without pause. This was Airi's special place, to which she would not bring someone who had not learned her special brand of etiquette. It took an average of two weeks. Most students ran away before that.

Airi spoke to Yosho, who was staring at the food. "The dishes here should be palatable to most people. What do you think?" Galaxy Academy hosted students from diverse backgrounds. Each nationality had its own taste in cuisine, and the rare students who went home unable to get used to the food did so mainly due to religious restrictions, not a matter of being "picky."

"Jurai was originally a multicultural nation, so I'm fine with cuisine from anywhere. I have no religious restrictions..."

"Okay, good." Airi said, visibly relieved, and they began eating. The food here tasted better than what was served in the dorms and felt homier.

"Airi-dono, are you the guide for others besides me?" Yosho asked between bites.

"No, just you right now... Oh, are you asking about the other guy from Jurai?" Airi took a sip of her tea. "I gave him my opinion, and he put in a request for someone else. And I've heard nothing since. Well, that kind of thing happens a lot to me."

"Is that so?" Yosho gazed at the chuckling Airi and figured the other Juraian was Amaki.

They continued to chat idly about their interests and hobbies, finished their meal, and rose to go to the cashier. "Yosho-kun, go on ahead. I'm going to pay the bill."

"I asked you out today, so I should..."

"Don't be silly. Students using government funds to study abroad shouldn't spend frivolously. Paying with money you're sponging off your parents doesn't give me any satisfaction."

"Aren't you in the same boat?"

"*I* have a part-time job. So I got this." She poked Yosho's forehead lightly with her index finger.

As Crown Prince, he owned his own planet and paid the tuition from the generated income. *If I told her it's my own money... she would probably hit me.* Airi would not accept that as earned income.

Airi paid the bill and walked over to Yosho, waiting by the entrance. "Sorry to keep you waiting... Let's go."

"Thank you for the meal."

"It's no big deal."

"May I ask a question?"

"What?"

"You said you had a job. Why? You're not in a situation where you have no choice, are you?"

"To be able to speak my own mind, I guess..."

"Your opinions?"

"And to have some freedom," Airi said, looking up at the fading daylight. She did not show it in her face, but Yosho sensed a little sadness from her.

"Isn't it hard to work while studying? And you're also my guide..."

"It's no big deal once you get used to the workload. And you don't require much fuss... But there is one problem."

"What? What have I done to cause you trouble?"

"You're such a good kid that I can't work my frustrations out on you." Airi clenched her fists and put them in the air like she'd done the first time they met at the space port.

"You seemed to have just done a lot of that at the park..."

"Ha ha! That was not nearly enough."

Hearing Airi's joyful laugh, Yosho laughed in spite of himself. "Maybe I should get a job, too."

"The quickest would be offering yourself up as an experimental subject."

"Airi-dono, you're not serious?!" He stopped in the street and stared at her.

"I'm not doing that. There's no telling *what* they'd do to me here. I tutor elementary students. There are three of them..." She suddenly remembered, as she quickly checked the time on her watch. "Uh-oh, in fact, it's almost time for that. I'm sorry, but I gotta go, Yosho-kun. I had fun today."

"Good luck on your job." They exchanged farewells and parted at the streetcar station.

Yosho saw the train off and felt a presence behind him. It was not malicious, but its focus was clearly directed at him. From the crowd, an elderly man slowly approached Yosho and reverently bowed his head. "Masaki Yosho Jurai-sama, I presume?"

"Yes. And you are?"

"I apologize for this sudden intrusion. My name is Hirata Kaneaki, butler to Amaki Kasen-sama. My master has ordered me to come get you."

Yosho noticed that the man was not alone and had placed about ten people around him. If he were to refuse, they would resort to force. Not even ten men would be able to hold Yosho down; he was that powerful already. They knew this, but their master's orders were absolute. Yosho could imagine how this faithful-looking man would take the blame for not being able to execute the order, and he felt compelled to accept the offer. "All right, please take me there."

The man who called himself Kaneaki was slightly taken aback at Yosho's docile words. He had never expected the Crown Prince to accept such a rude invitation. A large landcar pulled up in front of them, and Kaneaki opened the door for Yosho.

The stars started twinkling as they drove northward on the highway; Yosho sat in the backseat and spoke to Kaneaki sitting across from him. His face had reminded him of Kanemitsu, whom he had met on his first day here. "Excuse me, but are you related to Hirata Kanemitsu-dono?"

"My apologies. I should have come clean with you first.

Kanemitsu is my son. A couple of nights ago, he was extremely rude to you. What he did was entirely my responsibility..."

"Please don't worry about it. I am but a student here, and he gave me advice and encouragement as my senpai. I am still inexperienced, so please tell him I would appreciate more direction from him in the future." Yosho bowed deeply. He may have been Jurai Crown Prince, but even Kaneaki found it hard to believe that this was a twelve year old.

"I'm sorry I summoned you." Amaki Kasen, surprisingly sturdily built, came out to greet them. He was about seventeen, with a nervous look in his eyes that belied his physique. He seemed polite on the surface, but he quickly and arrogantly sat down again. Kaneaki looked more surprised than Yosho at this patronizing behavior.

"You are dismissed," Kasen ordered Kaneaki.

The old man standing next to Kasen noticed that Kaneaki was about to say something and held out his hand to reiterate the command to withdraw. Kaneaki glanced at Yosho and left the room. The old man saw him off and bowed reverently to Yosho. "Yosho-sama. I am grand chamberlain of Amaki Kasen-sama; my name is Kazakami Seishu. I am pleased to make your acquaintance. On this occasion..."

"Enough. Let's get started." Kasen, irritated, haughtily leaned back in his seat.

"Of course... We had you come here today due to my master's patriotism."

He's really going to make his chamberlain say everything? I see. No wonder Airi-dono didn't like Kasen. He started to realize how ridiculous this was, so he cut to the chase. "I understand what Kasen-dono is trying to say. But I plan to ask Airi-dono to continue to be my guide."

"Wh-what? She's the daughter of a hostile enemy leader. She mocked and humiliated me!" Kasen stood and raised his voice.

Unperturbed, Yosho answered, "There may be conflict between believers of Airain and some Juraians, but it hasn't developed into a hostile relationship yet."

"They take advantage of us because of such weakness!"

"It's forbidden to bring quarrels between nations to the Academy. We have gathered here to *study*. Where does that put the Academy, which provides us with this site? And people from various countries are here. Surely you're aware of what they would think of anyone with no sense of decorum." Yosho's voice was clear, without faltering.

"B-but a Crown Prince on a woman's leash is a national disgrace! What kind of effect would that have on Jurai?"

"I am still inexperienced enough that I need guidance from others. What kind of influence would I have? You shouldn't worry about someone who's not even allowed to attend the Supreme Council yet."

"Then what about the Royal Trees? The Crown Prince, tricked by a woman, could turn against us with a First Generation Tree."

What an absurd thing to say. Yosho could only laugh internally at Kasen's obstinate offensive. "I appreciate your concern, but the Royal Trees are sentient. Under contract with Tsunami the progenitor, the Royal Trees were promised to entwine their fates with Jurai and would never grow hostile even under orders."

"What about influence on Jurai? The First Empress will be placed in a difficult position." Kasen targeted Yosho's greatest weakness. This was probably his trump card, but Yosho was undaunted.

"I'm here to study and to find friendship. I can't arbitrarily decide for myself what the Supreme Council might proclaim in the future. I will bear your advice in mind, but I must follow the rules of the Academy. Is that all right?"

"But you should avoid indiscretions...!"

"The selection of a guide is voluntary, and I understand final assignments are made by the student council. Surely all background information was taken into consideration. And since I haven't received any instruction from Jurai, I have no reason to have her step down as my guide. That's what I've decided."

"Urk..." Kasen scowled. The grand chamberlain beside him looked relieved that Yosho had smoothed things over Kasen's discourtesy without making things worse.

"If that is all, I have curfew, so may I excuse myself?"

"Take him home!" Kasen spat out and retreated to an inner room. The poor grand chamberlain approached Yosho with an expression of dismay.

"Y-your Majesty, please forgive us for the repeated transgressions."

"I'm not bothered. I'm grateful that he gave me advice."

"Such kind words."

Yosho gently turned down an invitation to dinner and headed back to the dorm. He was used to bitter words from being on Jurai and had acquired the art of this reaction entirely out of his love for his mother. His kindness allowed him to feel that such things were no big deal.

The fireworks for that night's celebration (happening tonight, as usual) lit his face through the car's window. He stared out in silence and remembered Airi. He figured the act would lift his spirits. In fact, a smile spread on Yosho's lips.

Back in his room, he accessed Funaho in orbit. All First Generation Trees were able to access any computer on Jurai without requiring authorization first. "Seto-sama's would be best..." After some pondering, Yosho linked to Mikagami, Seto's Second Generation Tree, via Funaho. Seto's ability to gather and analyze information was superior to that of his father and that of the Emperor of Jurai's official intelligence bureau. Of course, only a few in the Imperial Family knew this, namely the Emperor, Misaki, and Funaho. Yosho would never have found out if he did not have a First Generation Tree.

He asked Mikagami to analyze the data he gathered today, behind Seto's back. An order from a First Generation Tree was prioritized unless it endangered the life of the sworn partner of the Royal Tree. That was how Yosho was able to pull off a stunt like this. The results came back almost instantaneously.

"That seemed *too* fast. Hm...?!" Looking at it closely, an amount of data far beyond what he gathered, from throughout the Academy, flowed into his terminal. He was momentarily taken aback, but thinking calmly, it was obvious. Seto was the best at gathering intelligence on Jurai. There was no way she would not have information on the entire Galaxy Academy, as well as the actions of Yosho, one of its students.

"Wow, it's raining spies." Yosho and Airi's actions today were unexpectedly effective. It had spurred some kind of action from most of the intelligence organizations that had marked them. If he told Airi everything, she might become paranoid, so he picked out only the ones that might present danger to her.

However, under those conditions, the professional intelligence bureaus did not present any risk at all, and the terrorists had all been marked through cooperation between the bureaus and the Academy. The most dangerous were the ones not marked, i.e. Kasen and his student minions. Academy students were guaranteed free rein and privacy, but pushing the envelope on the rules was not a good thing, and severe punishment awaited if anything happened. Such was student privilege here.

Seto should have information on that. Yosho tried to pick out information on just the students from the massive amount of data but noticed that it was wholly missing.

"The students were excluded from intelligence gathering? No…it was extracted knowing I would access it?" Considering Seto, the latter was more likely. "She wants me to do the essential work for myself. Strict as always… Or not. She extracted the data in a way that's obvious to me, after all." He had the impression that he was still wrapped around her finger.

He examined the data on Kasen he had gathered himself. Kasen undoubtedly hated doing things on his own. The grand chamberlain and Kaneaki were not in a position to express their opinions, but he did not think they would execute unreasonable orders to use force against Airi. It came down to the student minions…

I don't understand why they haven't dealt with Airi-dono directly. The night I arrived, the five students who attacked me were undoubtedly the sons of warriors serving the Amaki Family. If they had been brought here as attendants for Kasen, they would've taken action immediately and wouldn't report Kasen's orders to the Academy. They would probably make the excuse that they couldn't stand to have their friend insulted. I should assume that someone is holding them back…

He searched the list of students who came to study from Jurai last year, and his terminal displayed the personal data of six people. Yosho paused on Kanemitsu's name. *So there were six from last year including Kanemitsu. The other five… I knew it.* The other five were not related to Kasen. But there was no mistake that they were the five with Kanemitsu that night. *I'll have to confirm this tomorrow. But Kanemitsu-dono was trying to separate me from Airi-dono. Is it because they can't do anything with me around?*

This was highly likely *if* Kanemitsu had discovered that he was here with a camouflaged Funaho. With Yosho at Airi's side and under Funaho's protection, it would be like a national military guarding her. But just because Kanemitsu's father served Kasen did not mean the same for his son. The honest Kaneaki especially would not do that even under master's orders. The relationship between the Imperial Family and the warriors was a little different. Their status was not hereditary. If they felt no attraction to the master they served, they would leave, and it was the same when generations changed. Most of the warriors were effectively freelance. The Imperial Family member's competence determined how many distinguished warriors they could employ. Of course, some served over multiple generations purely in pursuit of special status.

Information was a difficult thing. He could come up with countermeasures by obtaining information, but his best options changed according to how much information his adversary had.

I feel like Seto-sama just gave me homework. That thought was so apt that he could not help but laugh.

Having promised to have lunch with Airi, Yosho hurried to the cafeteria when a student appeared to block his way. It was Hirata Kanemitsu. "You handled Kasen well."

"Did your father tell you, Kanemitsu-dono?"

"He won't give up so easily."

"I don't think there's any real danger, since you're holding him back."

"H-how did you know that?" Kanemitsu could not conceal how upset he was.

"I asked the five I met the other day, earlier this morning."

"Hmph, you certainly are thorough. But it will only get worse if you stay by her side. You can handle yourself, and I can hold them back when she's alone. But others have plans for when both of you are together."

"You mean the Imperial House Amaki?"

"Yes. Kasen is related to House Amaki."

That was why Kanemitsu-dono wanted to handle it himself. No, that was not it. *If so, why did Kasen-dono try to separate us so much? Leave us alone and he'd more likely be able to claim my actions were problematic. Is he trying to make it seem like his loyalty is toward me, to score a point with House Masaki?*

But it was a fact that Kasen was in contact with House Amaki...or specifically, Amaki Shuzan. The thirst for power had taken Shuzan, and he kept plotting against House Masaki. Yosho, whose father was the Emperor of Jurai and head of House Masaki, had been served political attacks (mostly verbal attacks) before. But this case seemed different from the way Shuzan usually did things. That gave Yosho slight pause.

What's going on...?

"There you are! You're late. What are you doing?" Airi's shrill voice interrupted Yosho's thoughts.

"Later." Kanemitsu patted his shoulder and hurriedly left. Perhaps he found Airi difficult to deal with.

Airi ran up to Yosho and stopped, looking at Kanemitsu walking away. "That's Kanemitsu-kun..."

"You know him?"

"My friend was his guide. I heard his grades are top-notch. But he finds girls difficult to talk to." She tittered as she remembered the rumors. "But Yosho-kun, you're an expert."

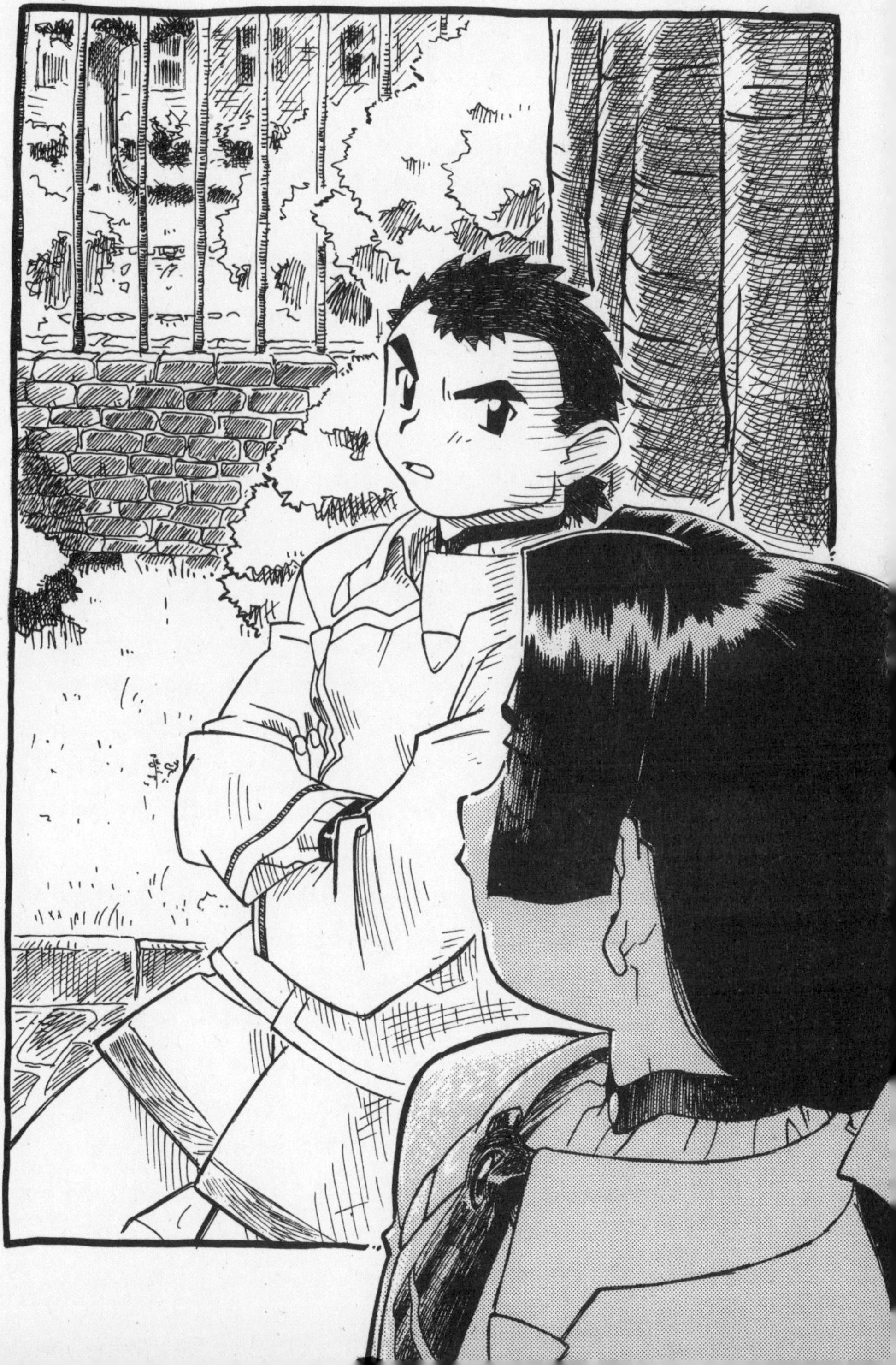

"At what?"

"Handling girls."

"That's not true. Sometimes I have no idea what they're thinking."

"That's not what I'm saying. You know, like how you make a girl wait." She looked at him provokingly, and Yosho finally understood.

"I'm sorry, Airi-dono. I'm late, but would you like to have lunch with me?"

"I guess." Belying her curt reply, Airi took Yosho's arm and walked to the cafeteria. Yosho liked her aggressive side, and it brightened his mood.

A few days passed without incident. Then one morning, things began to escalate with an anonymous e-mail sent to Yosho. It contained a message that could be taken either as a warning or a threat. It expressed that his interactions with Airi were not desirable. There were no clues as to the sender, and Kanemitsu confirmed that Kasen had not done anything. Yosho hurried to see Airi, and her unexpected indifference had him slightly confused.

"Oh, that e-mail? Yeah, I got it, too."

"Huh? Oh…"

"Don't look so serious. I get this kind of harassment often."

"Have you been in danger before?"

"Sometimes. So I know how to deal with it, don't worry. There's the Guardian System, too."

"You mean Kaunack?" This was the high-end GS maker run by the Academy.

"Yes, it's fully customized, tuned by each country's combat technician in tandem with Kaunack's engineers for each user's individual needs."

"Then please keep it set to the maximum level."

"It's not like we're going to a battlefield. We don't want to kill anyone by accident." Airi was appalled.

"Their reaction speed will be able to adjust to an ordinary attack."

"Don't make this into a big deal. Besides, I can't walk around all threatening like that. Walking in a crowd would set it off into alert mode and continuous pseudo-materialization. Thanks for your concern, but I got this," Airi said with a laugh, and Yosho's face clouded over.

Even a full-version GS wouldn't impede a top-rate Jurai fighter as long as they figure out the quirks in the programming. An Imperial Family member would be worse. If I could at least put Airi-dono's GS under Royal Tree control...

"What's with that face? You take things too seriously. If someone is actually after my life, they wouldn't be sending letters."

"What about when they realize you won't do as they demand?"

"Shall we part ways, then?"

"That's not my intent. I..." Yosho looked at Airi and was speechless. A tear fell down her cheek. "A-Airi-dono...?"

"So that's the world you live in. I can't speak for others, but..."

She sadly cast her eyes downward, then glanced over at him. As soon their eyes met, Yosho felt a chill...but then it was too late. "Arrrg! Being so high-strung will make you go bald!!" She pounced on Yosho and put him into another incomprehensible joint lock. This seemed to be her pattern.

"A-Airi-dono. People are watching. This isn't becoming..."

"Quiet!" They were in the courtyard. Passing students snickered at them, and people who knew Airi even called out to her to not bully him so much.

"A-Airi-dono..."

"Quit complaining!!"

Tangled up in Airi's joint lock, Yosho could hear joyful laughter, not only from the students, but laughter audible only to him. *Funaho...? Is that you? I see...you've taken a liking to Airi-dono. All right, thank you.*

A few minutes later, Yosho was sitting up, impassively fanning Airi, who had slumped to the ground panting, just like on their date. "Are you all right?"

"You're so irritating. Play along with me a little. I'm acting the idiot by myself!!"

"You are?"

"Stop that, you idiot!!" She jumped up to yell at Yosho, who impassively held out his hand. In it was a wooden ring. "What's this...?"

"It's a good luck charm. Please hold onto it."

"It's very pretty, but I can't accept this."

"Why not?"

"I can't take something so valuable without reason."

"No, I carved this myself. What looks like jewels is hardened tree sap. Good-quality ones are like charms back on Jurai."

"You carved this yourself?"

"Yes. You've taken such good care of me, so I would like you to have it."

Airi took it and put it on the ring finger on her right hand. She raised the back of her hand to show him. "Thank you. It makes me happy... Well?"

"Huh...?"

"Isn't there something else you say in these cases?"

"Oh, u-uh, it looks good on you."

"You sound very reluctant."

"No, it looks very good on you." Yosho repeated and laughed. Partly because Airi was not upset about the e-mails, and he was happy that she accepted the ring but also because the ring really did look good on her.

Airi held the ring up to the sun. "It's so pretty..." Yosho wondered about the expression on her face as she turned her back to him.

There were more anonymous e-mails, but they continued their lives at the Academy without paying much heed to them, as they were practically harmless. One day, there was a pounding at the door, almost breaking it down. It was eight o'clock at night, way past curfew.

"Yosho-kun, Yosho-kun, Yosho-kun! Come on out, Yosho!!"

The muffled voice of Airi was on the other side, so Yosho hurriedly opened the door.

"Airi-dono, what's the matter?!"

Airi grabbed him by the collar, her face twitching. "I-I-It was a…"

"What?"

"A voice! I couldn't tell if it was a man or a woman, and then some hooligans came out and…"

She was panicked and not making any sense. The students in other rooms heard the commotion and gathered to see what was going on. Yosho determined that inviting her into his room in these circumstances would only lead to gossip and decided to use the counseling room.

He placed a cup of tea on the table and looked at Airi sitting on the sofa. "Are you calmer now?"

"A little… Sorry, I was so shocked," Airi laughed weakly. Yosho was sure something must have happened for her to act in this unimaginably uncharacteristic way.

"What happened?"

"Well…" Airi started to explain about the events that just transpired.

After class, Airi was on her way home. The path through the park, usually full of pedestrian traffic, was deserted at the time. Right when she noticed that something was off, Airi's GS activated, and sparks flew between her Guardian and a black shadow.

"Who's there?!" There was no answer, but sparks continued

to fly here and there in the darkness. *What's going on? You've got to be kidding me.* She felt fear as she had never felt before. The opponent was invisible. Only the sparks as it clashed with her GS and the sound of plasma indicated its existence. She remembered Yosho's warning, and right when she tried to reset the GS to maximum level, she noticed shadows in front of her.

"We warned you." They spoke through mechanically synthesized sound.

"W-warning? You mean in the e-mail..."

"Stay away from him, or else..." After a heartbeat, the shadow raised its hand. The sword it held glowed a pale light.

Right when she thought she was done for...

"Get away from her!!" Someone's voice rang in her mind, and a Guardian she had never seen before knocked down the shadow. She could see it as it happened right in front of her.

"Impossible!!" The two shadows melted into the darkness. But even unseen, the unknown Guardian was clearly superior. The energy emitted was an order of magnitude beyond anything else. It was giving off pressure that could actually be felt. Right after a few sparks, silence suddenly fell again.

"You'll be all right now. He's gone."

"Wh-who are you?" She forced the words from her lips into the darkness. She was shocked, but there was strangely no fear.

The voice started giggling and then broke into a laugh as it called Airi's name over and over before eventually fading far away. Airi was left alone in the park.

By the time she finished explaining, Airi was back to her usual self, perhaps due to the sense of security of being next to Yosho. "...And so I came here wondering if you had done something!!" She slammed on the desk in her usual way, pressing on Yosho.

"Are you hurt?"

"No! Just answer me!! What *was* that?!"

"Well, I mean..."

"It has to do with the ring you gave me, right?! I figured it was going to be something like that, but I thought, could it mean anything else if I was wrong... I mean, shadows attacking me, and a weird voice!!"

"Were you scared?"

"Huh?"

"Were you more scared of the voice than the attackers?"

"Why?"

"You seemed to be in quite a panic."

"Not at all...!" Airi declared. The fear had been blown away, only left with curiosity about the voice.

It's so typical of her... Yosho laughed internally, and she leaned closer. "Wh-what is it?"

"It wasn't male or female, not young or old... It *tickled*. Oh... you know, I love dogs." She started a non sequitur.

"Dogs...?"

"Especially bouncy puppies. And it felt like I was being swarmed by a herd of puppies... That's how it felt." She clasped her hands in front of her, euphoric, and Yosho finally understood.

"I see. So that's how that was related..." He could not tell her about Funaho right now, but he doubted she would let this go peacefully in this excited state. He still tried for the time being, "It's gotten late already today, so…"

"No!"

"I figured…" He knew how she would answer, but this flat-out refusal was tiring. *It is…too early to go to sleep yet. I have no choice, I suppose.* Yosho resolved to take her to Funaho. "All right. But we can't talk here. So…" There was no telling who was watching.

He whispered into her ear, and she grinned, "I knew it was your fault!"

Yosho smiled wryly.

Puppy Funaho

THE LAST FLIGHT HAD DEPARTED from the space port, and the lights were on, but there were few people out and about. Yosho arrived at the lobby using Funaho's terminal, felt a presence in the designated area, and cheerfully called out, "Sorry to keep you waiting."

Airi appeared from behind the pillar. "Looks like you made it out."

"Yes, but I passed by other students on the way, and I was surprised that nobody questioned me."

"Ha ha! There isn't anyone tactless enough to say something to interfere with someone who managed to outwit the dorm night check. Of course, that doesn't mean you get a free pass. Well, someone will warn you if you're someplace you're *really* not supposed to be. In that case, you get the heck out of there, as told. Or else a guard will catch you. Or if you play it wrong, some shifty harvesters will catch you."

"Harvesters?"

"People out looking for human experimental subjects. It doesn't matter. Hurry up."

"You're the one who brought it up. This way." They headed to Funaho's gate, where she returned to the space port from orbit (though the port data had been tampered with so that it seemed like she had never left). Through a passage lit only by emergency lights, they boarded Funaho and arrived on the main bridge.

Airi looked around at the bridge and said, "Yosho-kun, I hope you're not going to tell me that the voice was this ship's computer."

"What?" Yosho was bewildered that she had hit the nail on the head.

"You're not serious, are you?"

"You are correct."

"I'm leaving!" She squared her shoulders and stomped away, and Yosho hurriedly held her back.

"W-wait. You came all the way out here."

"When I heard that voice, I really got my hopes up. But it's just a computer?" Airi sounded angry, but she looked deeply disappointed.

"A-Airi-dono, what were you hoping for?"

"A Royal Tree... Children of Tsunami, the powerful and intelligent progenitor and guardian god of the Jurai Imperial Family..."

"I see."

There was a laugh, and Airi looked up. "Yosho-kun, don't you laugh..."

The laughter continued directly into their minds, just like at the park. "Airi... Airi."

"This voice..."

"It's the one you were hoping for." In that instant, they were transported to the *real* main bridge, the Hall of Royal Trees. The stifling scent of wet soil and summer grass was thick in the pure, sweet air. The whole place danced with light and sound. Spheres of light wove exuberantly between the tree branches, flickering in time to a faint melody. As if the Tree in front of them were singing...

Airi opened her eyes wide. "Yosho-kun, are you serious...?"

"Allow me to introduce you to Funaho, a First Generation Imperial Tree." The sphere of light proliferated, intensifying the brightness.

"Hello, hello, Airi. Airi..." The spheres of light crowded and fluttered about Airi.

"Oh!!" With a sigh of wonder, Airi dropped to her knees. "Please tell me, what are you?" She implored the light.

Yosho could not help but be shocked at her desperate cry. "Airi-dono, what's the matter?"

"Is Tsunami the Progenitor one of the Three Goddesses?!" Not listening to Yosho, Airi looked up at Funaho with her hands clasped in front of her chest, as if imploring the gods. Visually, it looked like the Advent.

Suddenly, the light disappeared, and silence fell around them. As if that was Funaho's answer to Airi's question. "Funaho... Funaho-sama! Please answer me!!"

"Airi, Airi-dono!!" Yosho embraced Airi, her hands outstretched, to hold her back. "Airi-dono!!"

"Yosho...kun... I..." Her shoulders slumped. Airi hung her head.

Supporting her, Yosho led her towards the bench by the side of the nursery Unit. Airi was breathing heavily, unable to contain her excitement and distress. "Are you all right?"

"Yes, I'm sorry... I'm sorry..."

"What were you trying to ask the Royal Tree? If you don't mind..." Airi would not answer. "Airi-dono?"

"I want to find God..." After a pause, she started talking slowly. It was a confessional.

"God?"

"Yes, the Three Goddesses, if possible."

"The Three Goddesses?"

"Yes, or rather, intelligent beings of a higher dimension... They are often called gods even in this modern technologically advanced age, due to their awesome power. Especially..."

"When it pertains to religion."

"That's right. There have been several confirmed examples, but they hardly ever show themselves to humanity. I found out through research at the Academy that there have only been twenty-eight encounters, including scientifically reliable accounts discovered in the ruins of pre-historical civilizations. But among the super-powerful intelligent beings of a higher dimension, there seemed to be three Goddesses with singular abilities who are an order of magnitude more powerful than the rest."

"There seemed?"

"Yes, through methodical classification of accounts from those civilizations, they can be grouped into three types."

"That's rather vague. Is there not enough information?"

"No. These instances of other-dimensional intelligent beings have specifics. Otherwise they wouldn't be accepted as true encounters."

"Then..."

"The data exists," she interrupted. "Data that can't be accepted."

"Can't be accepted?!"

"Yes, it exists, but then it doesn't. It doesn't exist, but we can see it. Those are the clear descriptions left behind." Airi looked at him, waiting for his words.

"Light Hawk Wings..."

Airi nodded silently. The Light Hawk Wings were not detectable in any energy readings, but they were visible as light. She was saying that the wings of light that the Royal Trees above Third Generation could generate were the manifestations of the Three Goddesses. "Sometimes science has cruel results. The act of pursuing the truth can crush you. The gods were stripped of their veils of romanticism and lost the power they held in people's hearts. And now people have to fill those holes themselves. Gods are eternal, but people are not. No matter how great their charisma, once a person is gone, they're no longer a god."

"Are you talking about the first leader of Airain?"

"My great-grandfather made Airain the most powerful religion in the galaxy. But to maintain it once it got too large, a powerful idol was vital. The council first sought that in blood lineage. They set up my grandfather, then my father, to replace my influential great-grandfather's charisma. But as more internal factions grew within the council, this was no longer possible. They tried to create a new god by deifying my great-grandfather, but that can only be done when the god in question has absolute power. So the council wanted an absolute idol, a god… They wanted Tsunami-sama."

"…!!" It was a shocking confession.

"There are almost no Airai believers on Jurai. But that's obvious. They have a real god on Jurai. So the council wanted to propagate Airain on Jurai, and make Tsunami-sama into an Airai god."

"You too, Airi-dono…?"

"I thought so while I was on Airai—that Tsunami-sama must be Airai's god. That Jurai was monopolizing Tsunami-sama for themselves." This was her confessional. It became hard for Airi to look Yosho in the eye, and she averted her gaze "But I got here, and met so many people, and the ones from countries I used to dislike or look down on were so nice to me. It destroyed my sense of values. I was embarrassed for what I tried to do and the lies the council taught. It's laughable. They were trying to protect the organization, but at some point that had become the goal. They even went against their own teachings. And it's all because they didn't have a real god."

"That's why they wanted Tsunami?"

"Tsunami-sama belongs to Jurai. It would only sow seeds of discord to claim her. So I thought another one of the goddesses would work just as well. I thought Tsunami-sama would know something… But it's no use. Funaho-sama has also forsaken me…"

Airi covered her face with her hands and cried stifled sobs. Yosho gently stroked her hair, feeling for Airi, trapped between her country and her friends, and driven to an emotional cliff.

Funaho felt the same. "Airi... Airi, don't cry..." Her voice that spoke to their minds was sad, sympathizing with Airi.

"...?!" Airi slowly raised her face to look at Funaho.

"Airi-dono. Tsunami is not a god," Yosho said. "Even if she has that much power, she can't be the kind of god you espouse, and that's not what she would want. The person who met Tsunami and became the first leader of Jurai was said to have stated, 'We became friends.'"

"Friends? With Tsunami-sama?"

"Airi...don't cry..." Airi signaled that she was fine to a worried Funaho.

"Airi-dono, it's the same for Funaho and me. We became friends... And she didn't forsake you. She was just surprised. You suddenly went down on your knees, so she...let's say, ducked away to take cover, like a puppy...and then she peeked out to make sure you were all right."

"Airi, Airi...don't cry...Airi." The waves of pure sadness Funaho felt for Airi slowly but surely melted the heavy weight she had felt on her shoulders for so long. "Airi, Airi..."

"Don't cry, Funaho... I feel better now...okay?" Airi wiped her tears and was now trying to comfort Funaho in turn.

"Are you sure? Airi won't cry?"

"I'm fine," Airi smiled.

"Airi smiled," Funaho giggled, the ticklish waves of joy

widening the smile on Airi's lips. The beautiful lights had begun dancing again.

"Funaho, it's so pretty."

"Airi smiled. Airi..."

Airi raised her hands, and the spheres of light swarmed her. Funaho was not a god. But the light surrounding her seemed godly.

That usually takes a while... Yosho could not help but smile at them. The melody started slowly. The song of trees sung by Funaho enveloped Airi.

"Yosho-kun... Hey, Yosho-kun!"

"Hm... Airi-dono?" Yosho forced open his eyes, shaken awake by Airi.

"Are you awake now?" Airi laughed and poked his cheek mischievously.

"Please stop..." Now he was wide awake. The morning sun shining into the bridge was hitting his cheek...which meant he had fallen asleep some time during Airi and Funaho's endless laughter. He finally came to his senses and bolted upright.

"Thanks, Yosho-kun. I feel better now. I don't have any answers yet, but at least I feel free to think. I'm sorry it got so late that it's morning now. Ha ha."

"I-I'm sorry. I should've kept watch."

"I'm fine. I filed an application for an overnight stay before I left. But you..."

"It's no problem. I left a dummy behind, and there's no roll call in the morning."

"Is that one where you can only bluff that you're in your own room?"

"No, it's under Funaho's control, so it's a hologram."

"Then make it so you went out. Let's grab breakfast somewhere... Oh, could I use the shower first?"

"Then I'll get your outfit cleaned and get a change of clothes ready. We can eat here if you'd like."

"Well...okay, maybe we should," Airi answered after a short pause to think.

"Then let's go to the living quarters." They transported off the bridge and went down the passage built against the trunk of the giant tree in the middle of the residential quarters. There was a forest, a river, a lake and hills, and a vast field filled with crops. The view was of a rural countryside.

Airi murmured, stunned, "Wh-where are we?"

"This is a residential area affixed in subspace... Ow!"

Airi had pinched Yosho's cheek. "Looks like this isn't a dream."

"Aren't you supposed to pinch your own?"

"Well, you were looking so proud, I couldn't help myself... But how is such a huge space affixed in a tiny cruiser... Is Funaho doing this?"

"Yes. This place has a diameter of 100 kilometers. The Second Generation Trees can affix a space up to the size of ten planets, but we have no idea what the maximum limit is for a First Generation Tree. But this is a personal space, and it would be meaningless to make it arbitrarily large, so this is what I have... What's wrong?"

"You deserve to be proud of that... What an incredible friend," She could only laugh at this point.

"We've been waiting for you, Airi-sama." The door opened and they were welcomed by a force field hologram dressed as a lady-in-waiting.

"Thanks! So this is your room, Yosho-kun?" Flabbergasted by the solemn wooden building, she breathed a sigh of admiration.

"You're the daughter of a religious leader. Why would this be shocking to you?" Yosho stubbornly protested at her persistent surprise.

"Nobody on Airai has a private room with a garden 100 kilometers square in subspace... Are you mad now?" She chuckled.

"No, not really..."

"I like the buildings on Jurai. They look very natural and dignified. It makes you feel at home. I like those of our churches that reuse old ruins, but the modern ones are really flashy, so..." Airi stuck her tongue out shyly.

"This way, please." The lady-in-waiting led her to the guest bathroom.

"Then I guess I'll help myself."

"Take your time."

Airi walked a couple steps and turned around. "You better not..."

"I won't peep."

"You could freak out a little. You're no fun..." Airi grumbled.

He gazed upon the pastoral scenery that stretched as far as the eye could see. *Well, it was rather gaudy.* He remembered the extremely colorful main shrine he had seen in the data files, which could not be called beautiful by any standard, and headed to his own bathroom.

"Yosho-kun! Hey, Yosho-kun!!" Yosho had finished first and had been waiting on the terrace, when Airi burst out from the guestroom in Juraian clothes. With her hair down, she looked so different that he was mesmerized. "What's the matter?"

"Nothing. It looks good on you."

"Y-you think so? Thanks... No! I mean, this!!" She seemed momentarily bashful but went back to her usual shouting self, holding the fabric in her fingertips.

"Was it not to your liking? I'm afraid it's..."

"That's not it. This is Juraian raw silk, isn't it? The finest, too... I've only ever seen it on church leaders. It feels so nice..." She stroked the fabric, enjoying its texture. Juraian raw silk was made in the exact same way as silk on Earth, but it was much finer and more durable. High-quality Juraian silk was translucent, and its color changed depending on the diet of the silkworms. It was produced in other countries as well, but the quality was inevitably inferior, and there were fewer colors available.

"It must be more expensive when you get as far out as Airai. This silk was made on board this ship. If you like it, please, keep it."

"Really? Heh heh..." Airi blissfully rubbed her cheek with the sleeve.

"Quality silk will last a long time if you treat it right. There's only so much I can use by myself, so I have quite a lot of raw silk stock. If you're in need of fabric, I can share as much as you want. I can also sew..." He noticed that Airi was brooding over this with clearly mixed feelings, intuited that she was hesitating because of the cost, and added, "How about market price on Jurai?"

"How much?"

"Let's see..." They talked in whispers for some reason.

"No way! Really? I'll buy it! I'm so happy! What should I make?" Airi hopped with joy at the conclusion of the negotiations. What Yosho was producing was the finest class of silk, worth more than Airi would have been able to afford. But Funaho took care of everything here, so there were no labor expenses nor need for a profit margin. Frankly, he could have given it away for free. He asked for a market price for something of ordinary quality that Airi would see as reasonable and affordable.

"Shall we have breakfast?"

"Oh yeah, I was on cloud nine and totally forgot. Say, maybe I should've asked earlier, but isn't the interior of a Royal Ship top secret?"

"Yeah, it's too late," Yosho smiled wryly. "Well, the residential quarters are my personal space, so anyone I invite is no problem. Only people the Royal Tree accepts can enter the bridge, but that means if the Royal Tree allows it, not even the Emperor of Jurai could forbid entry. It's top secret to protect the ships of the Fourth Generation and beyond, which are not sentient."

"If not even the most powerful person on Jurai can interfere, they must be truly special." Even if Royal Trees were not gods, what Airi had witnessed was truly unique.

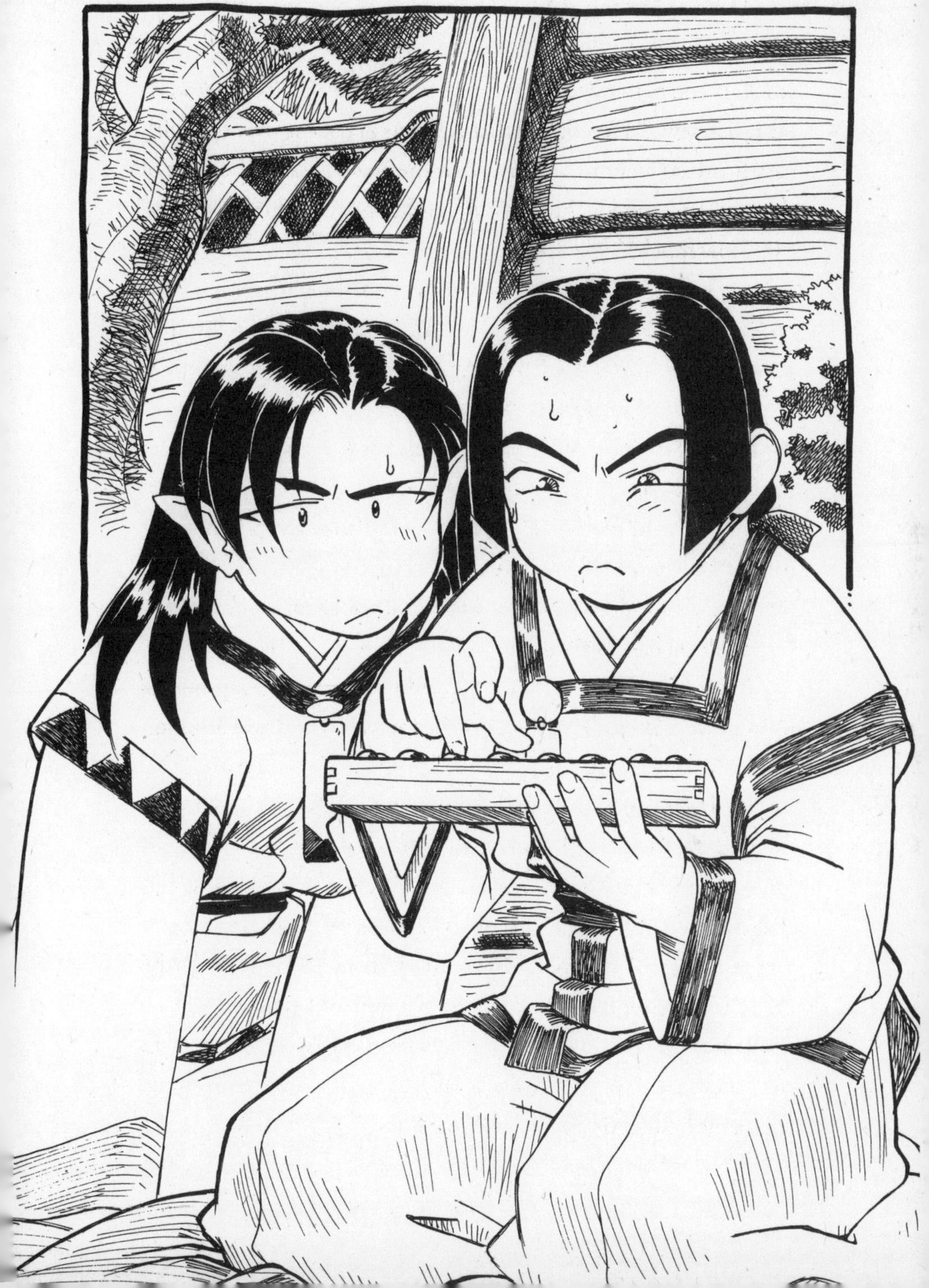

"If you get into a fight and make them mad, sometimes they won't let you in."

"What...?"

"But they usually break down and talk to you when they get lonely."

"Heh... I get it. I can totally see that. Ha ha ha!!" Airi remembered how Funaho acted like a puppy in the Hall of Royal Trees and laughed out loud, Yosho smiling with her. Funaho got jealous and started talking to them, of course, so their laughter grew even louder.

Later, Kasen fled to Jurai after only three months of study. The minions who were left behind merged into Kanemitsu's group and finally got to focus on their studies. Yosho grew to be able to talk to them normally, but he could never understand Kasen's intent. Harassment of Airi and Yosho ceased, and peaceful days continued; even Kanemitsu, who had given them so many warnings, never brought her up again.

Did I handle this well...? Yosho questioned himself over the homework that Seto had manipulated data to give him. It was too simple. He thought there may have been something he had overlooked and reached for the terminal, but there was no clue or even a sign of trouble. It did not take long for the question to become buried in a corner of his memories because campus life with Airi was fun. Before he knew it, six months had passed.

"Good morning, Airi-senpai."

"Good morning, Yosho-kun." It was their usual morning greeting, but it was very different from that of six months ago. Whether as the result of Airi's persistent education, or the relatively free vibe of the Academy, Yosho had become more boyish, and the difference from before was clear. It had taken him weeks to grow accustomed to addressing her this way. Of course, whenever he called her senpai, she was afraid that a part of her deep inside was awakening to something... She realized that he seemed different from usual. "What's wrong?"

Yosho scratched his head, hesitant, but he knew he had to come out and say it, so he opened his tightly pursed lips.

It was about the communication he had received from Jurai last night, from Seto.

"You look well, Yosho-dono."

"We haven't talked in a while. I'm glad you're well, too, Seto-sama."

"Thank you. I've heard that you've been very busy. We've heard the rumors all the way in Jurai." Seto stared at Yosho with her usual elegant countenance. She was not angry, but Yosho felt her gaze to be terrifying, and she had subtly placed an emphasis on the "busy" part. It was clear she knew everything.

Yosho knew he needed to come clean first and quickly spoke, "Seto-sama, I carefully considered how to handle the matter of Airi-dono in my own way..." He desperately tried not to let her notice that his voice was shaking. He did not feel guilty, and he regretted nothing. But when faced with Seto, the relaxation of six months here blew away like a feather. "I'm well prepared for a lecture, but..." He had summoned up the courage to say this much when the pressure of her eyes melted away. Yosho looked at Seto anew as if a spell were broken.

"Oh, nobody is mad about that. The Emperor of Jurai is extremely pleased that your efforts as a goodwill exchange student have been better than expected. All the visiting ambassadors have been talking about you."

Yosho knew, looking at her satisfied smile, that she had been teasing him. It was a bad habit of hers to shave years off someone's life like this. Yosho sulked, pouting his lips, and looked away.

Seto chuckled with her sleeve against her mouth, more than satisfied. She teased him because this was the expression she wanted to see. According to Seto, this sulky expression was the thing about him that resembled Azusa, the Emperor of Jurai, the most.

What a nuisance... He was well within his rights to think so. "Seto-sama, was that all?"

"I called you today to bring you word of the order from Azusa-sama, Emperor or Jurai."

"From Father?"

It was...

"What? An order to go home?!" Airi could not help but raise her voice. "You're not coming back?"

"I will. My father ordered me to fulfill my duties as Crown Prince on Jurai for six months out of the year."

"Then you'll be back in six months?"

"Yes, I will."

"I see..." Airi let out a sigh of relief. Nobody noticed that her expression grew slightly firmer as the day of his departure approached. It was a subtle difference she did not even realize herself.

The day before he left, Yosho looked for Airi to say goodbye, but he could not find her anywhere. Her friends had also been looking for her, and they went to all the places they knew, to no avail. He reluctantly went to pay his respects to others, and it was night by the time he went to see Kanemitsu last of all. He walked down the dorm hallway and almost bumped into a man as he rounded a corner.

"Excuse me, Masaki-kun..." The man nodded lightly and left. Yosho did not know him, but he was a lecturer for the students a grade above him, and remembered that he had seen him with Kanemitsu a number of times. This was a student dorm, but teachers often came and went, so Yosho paid no heed and continued to Kanemitsu's room. Before, he would have noticed the slight change in his attitude, his hostility and scorn. But the six months of living here had cast a fog over his instincts.

"Kanemitsu-dono, it's Yosho." The intercom by the door gave him permission to enter, and the door opened.

"Masaki-dono, it's you. What's the matter? Don't you leave tomorrow?"

"Well, I wanted to pay my respects."

"You didn't have to come all the way here. You're serious to a fault. If the Crown Prince of Jurai is leaving, you can be sure everyone will see you off tomorrow."

"I'll be back in six months, so that's really not necessary."

"The others are fond of you. Well, there's nothing wrong with seeing off a friend. Is that why you're here?"

"I came to ask you a favor." He did not have much time, so he went straight to the point.

"Guard Airi...? Is that what you want me to do?"

"Not really guard, but can you watch out for her?" Yosho bowed deeply.

"Wh-why are you asking me...? I told you before to stay away from her." Kanemitsu argued, confounded. Even if they had become friends, Yosho was the son of his country's sovereign.

"You're the one who held people back from harassing her."

"It wasn't a personal grudge. And Juraian warriors don't harass non-combatant women."

"I'm counting on you."

"No. I can't. I'm returning to Jurai in a few days."

It did not escape Yosho's notice that Kanemitsu's expression darkened. "Why? The study abroad is for a minimum of two years, and I heard you were staying to get your master's degree."

"Hmph...! I can see why you got the order to go home," Kanemitsu said sarcastically.

"What do you mean?"

"I feared you the way you were before."

"Feared?"

"Yeah. You were just a kid, but also like a sharpened blade, with eyes that saw everything. Not a sham like Kasen. Small, but a wolf befitting the Imperial Family... Airi Magma sure is something. I guess she tamed that wolf. In that sense, she was no delicate flower herself, befitting the daughter of a head of state. It was just supposed to scare her a little back then, but I got too fired up..." Kanemitsu was not acting like his usual self.

"Kanemitsu-dono?!" Just as Yosho began to ask, Kanemitsu's figure blurred. Leaving afterimages behind, he slashed at Yosho.

Yosho instinctively blocked with the button on the sleeve of his uniform. The swordsmanship was not at all like Kanemitsu's previous feats but more like an adult warrior.

"Impressive," Kanemitsu said. "You've lost your touch, yet you blocked it easily. But how would you have handled it before?"

"...?!"

Kanemitsu was right. Before, Yosho would not have even had to parry the attack. Even if Kanemitsu's slash was that of a warrior's, Yosho would have imperceptibly moved his upper body at a speed faster than what could be recognized. Fast enough to seem like Kanemitsu's sword had passed through his body. He did not do that not out of carelessness, but because his focus had dulled. He knocked the sword away, moved back to a distance, and yelled, "Impossible. Are you the one who attacked Airi-senpai...?"

"Hey, you know my father serves Kasen. And the Amaki Family is related to the Imperial House Amaki. The answer is simple."

He remembered the expression on the lecturer he ran into. That sneer had been in anticipation of what was to happen here. "I didn't expect this kind of answer. That lecturer..."

"My contact. They're excessively cautious when they contact

me. He was giving me the orders from House Amaki, and I was giving my report."

"Kanemitsu-dono! Are you sure you want to be saying these things…?"

"You're concerned about a spy, *now*? I betrayed you."

"I thought you didn't have a choice, considering your father's position…"

"Feh… I can see how Airi thinks you deserve a punch. Be more selfish!"

"You could ask Seto-sama to protect you and Kaneaki-dono…"

Kanemitsu abruptly punched him in the face. "You idiot! A Juraian warrior could never do that! What a disgrace! My dad and I haven't sunk so low that you need to worry about us! You're the one whose standing is shaky. It'll be ten thousand years before you've come far enough to worry about me!!"

"But…"

"Don't worry, he wouldn't make me do anything important. Come to think of it, he never specified who the orders came from."

"Are you saying it's possible it's not House Amaki?"

"Who knows? I certainly don't care. It's true that he kept mentioning my father." Kanemitsu seemed to say this on purpose, but it seemed clear that it had to do with House Amaki.

"About Kaneaki-dono…"

"Dad isn't that weak. He's there through his own convictions." Kanemitsu cut off Yosho.

"I'm sorry."

"You don't know this, but Dad is a well-known warrior… If

I'm ever worried about him, he smacks me. 'Worry about your own dang self.' He even broke my tooth once! I'll *never* worry about him! So don't you worry about him, either. He said I'm no longer needed. He told me I'm free to do what I want, even if it was to tell you the truth. I failed to pull you apart from Airi, so there's no more reason for them to keep me here... And you have other problems."

"It's not like I hadn't thought about it before. House Masaki..."

"Well, it's a real nuisance."

"I'm sorry. But why did House Amaki try to separate me and Airi-senpai?"

"The underlings never understand what their bosses want."

"I see. You would think it would be more convenient for them if I stayed with Airi-dono. It shouldn't have been a problem to try to pull us apart openly rather than subversively."

"Who knows? You know better than I do. I have no idea. But it means what's at stake is more complicated than we could imagine. He told me to watch the others so they don't harass Airi. So don't worry about her." Kanemitsu seemed to have gotten it all out of his system, reverting to his usual demeanor.

"I heard you wanted to get a master's degree here. I don't want to pry, but..."

"Then don't. I was an idiot to depend on others. I appreciate your sentiment, as a friend."

"Okay..."

"I'll make them acknowledge me, one day. Like Utsutsumi-sama." The head of House Kamiki, Utsutsumi, used to be a warrior, but he united the unaffiliated pirates and warriors with his superior skills and made people acknowledge the addition of a thirteenth army among the "Twelve Divine Generals" serving House Kamiki at the time. "He's amazing. He married the woman known as Jurai's demon princess... And he's the father of Misaki-sama."

Yosho's cheeks flushed at Misaki's name.

"Speaking of that demon princess... Someone wanted a lock of her hair. What's the story behind it?"

"Is that what they said? It all started a long time ago, during the battle with the pirate's guild." That was the war where Seto had earned her nickname. "Seto-sama gave locks of her hair as good luck charms to the new recruits. And they all returned alive. That started the trend of carrying locks of hair from powerful or lucky people."

"That sounds like Seto-sama."

"Misaki-sama is the only one who won all seven championships of the Jurai martial arts. She's especially popular among the warriors." Kanemitsu looked at the clock. The time was close to roll call. "You return home tomorrow... You'd better get going."

"I'm sorry I overstayed my welcome. We may be able to meet again on Jurai. Stay well until then." Yosho held out his hand, and Kanemitsu reflexively shook it. At that moment, he transferred the invisible guardian summoning diagram on his to Kanemitsu's. It was not likely that anything would happen to him, but there was no guarantee.

I'm sure he'll tell me to butt out... He could not hand over a terminal to Funaho like he'd done with Airi, and though a lot inferior to a Guardian controlled by Funaho, Kanemitsu and his warrior strength would be able to handle most situations.

Kanemitsu saw Yosho out of the room.

"It's roll call already. I didn't get to see Airi-dono...!" He then remembered that there was one last place she could be that he had not looked yet, and instead of returning to the dorm, went to the space port. He boarded Funaho and ran to the Hall of Royal Trees. Airi was there.

"What are you doing...?"

There were an incredible number of puppies running around. Yosho approached Airi, who was in bliss, surrounded by those puppies. "Um..."

"Oh, there you are. Finally." Airi's tone was cold. "And here I thought that you would notice sooner. Right, babies?" She was the picture of a wife making a sarcastic comment to a husband too busy to pay attention to her... But Yosho, being thirteen (he'd aged a year while he was at the Academy) could not understand what she was trying to say, and Airi did not expect him to. She was enjoying a self-contained, grown-up joke against a younger boy.

"I'm sorry. Are these puppies Funaho?"

"Yes. I wanted to do this just once. You took so long coming here, so I figured this was the perfect opportunity." Airi giggled and hugged a puppy hologram created by Funaho. Funaho reacted to her joy, and the puppies charged Yosho and Airi en masse. The two were covered in puppies.

"H-hey, Funaho!!"

"Ha ha ha ha ha!!" Bombarded by the soft, cuddly puppies and Funaho's ticklish emotional wave, Airi was in a trance. In the middle of this puppy mob, Airi and Yosho momentarily touched, skin to skin. Airi vowed not to forget the feeling. *I'll make sure to remember until he comes back in six months.*

"Yosho-kun... C'mon, Yosho-kun!"

"Hm... Airi-dono?" Shaken awake, Yosho opened his eyes slightly.

"Are you awake?" Airi laughed and poked his cheek mischievously.

"Please stop!!" He was now fully awake.

"This is the same as last time... It's morning already, ha ha." The sunlight shining through the bridge was hitting their faces... which meant that they had fallen asleep here again. Except it was more like they passed out. "I brought a change of clothes to see you off, so can I use the shower?"

"Then we'll have breakfast in my room again."

"Okay," Airi answered with a smile, extended her hand, and grabbed Yosho's. He would normally balk and protest, but just for this moment, it felt like the right thing to do.

He pulled her hand as he walked. "Let's go to my living quarters."

Kanemitsu

Yosho woke to the sound of leaves rustling and Misaki moving about the outer wall of Tenju. *It's morning already. I didn't sleep very well.* It had been a week since he came back to Jurai, and he was still not physically used to the tension and circadian rhythm on Jurai. It was exhausting to deal with Ayeka and Misaki, who happily romped around on being able to see Yosho again. He realized that his senses had dulled physically and mentally more than he had thought and was acutely aware of why Seto had brought him back after only six months. Strangely, he had gotten over his feelings for Misaki. There were days in the final three months at the Academy when he did not even remember her.

Well... I was busy, and Airi-dono had filled up the rest of my free time, so I didn't have the time to be sentimental.

"Good morning, Yosho-chan... I mean, Yosho-dono." Misaki made her way inside his room, which was unusual.

"Misaki-sama?!"

"Were you still asleep? Come on, get up. You have places to go."

Yosho clutched his covers so they would not be ripped off him and asked, "Did I have plans today?"

"Official business for House Kamiki, but Mother suddenly said to bring you, too."

"Seto-sama?"

"Yes. Come on, hurry!"

"All right…please don't pull." He shooed Misaki out of his room, got ready, and headed to Jurai Imperial Academy as specified by Seto. That day, there was a ceremony to send off the cadets on a training voyage, and since Utsutsumi was an alumni, he attended every year. The white yukigasumi, or Powder Snow flowers, which resembled cherry blossoms on Earth, were in full bloom.

"I look forward to this view every year." Walking the vast gardens on the way to campus, Seto was entranced. Next to her, Utsutsumi maintained a stony silence.

Yosho walked between them, looked sidelong at a grouchy Utsutsumi, and asked Seto, "Seto-sama, why bring me here today?"

Seto ignored Yosho and looked at her husband. "Dear, I'm going to take Yosho-dono and Misaki on an errand. You go on ahead."

"Hm, but I was going to show him around. Shouldn't we introduce him to the faculty here?" Utsutsumi answered in a dignified voice.

Seto smiled scornfully and said, "Why don't you do that after the send-off ceremony?"

"Azusa... I mean, the Emperor used to attend here. Some want to see his son." A hint of panicked impatience was in Utsutsumi's voice.

"Then shall I accompany you, Utsutsumi-sama?" Yosho suggested, as from Utsutsumi's attitude and Seto's meaningful expression, he figured that something was up, and for reasons unclear to him determined that he should side with Utsutsumi.

Utsutsumi returned a smile of relief at his proposal. "All right, then come with me. I'll show you all the interesting places."

"Thank you, Utsutsumi-sama."

"How admirable of you, Yosho-dono." Of course, Seto knew what he was thinking. "But I'm afraid this must be done before the ceremony."

"Then we'll go ahead. You go do the errand."

"This has to do with Yosho-dono, dear." Seto attacked him as if she were peeling one finger off at a time as he clung desperately on a cliff.

"All right, then I'll go with you." Just as Utsutsumi said this, Misaki appeared behind him and grabbed him. Seto took Yosho's shoulders tightly.

"Yosho-chan...this is where he molested me." Seto appealed with tears in her eyes. Needless to say, this was a false claim.

"F-for decency's sake!!" Utsutsumi yelled red-faced, abandoning all pretense of dignity he had so desperately composed. No matter how he struggled, Misaki did not budge in her bear hug. Sadly for him, Misaki was more physically powerful than her father.

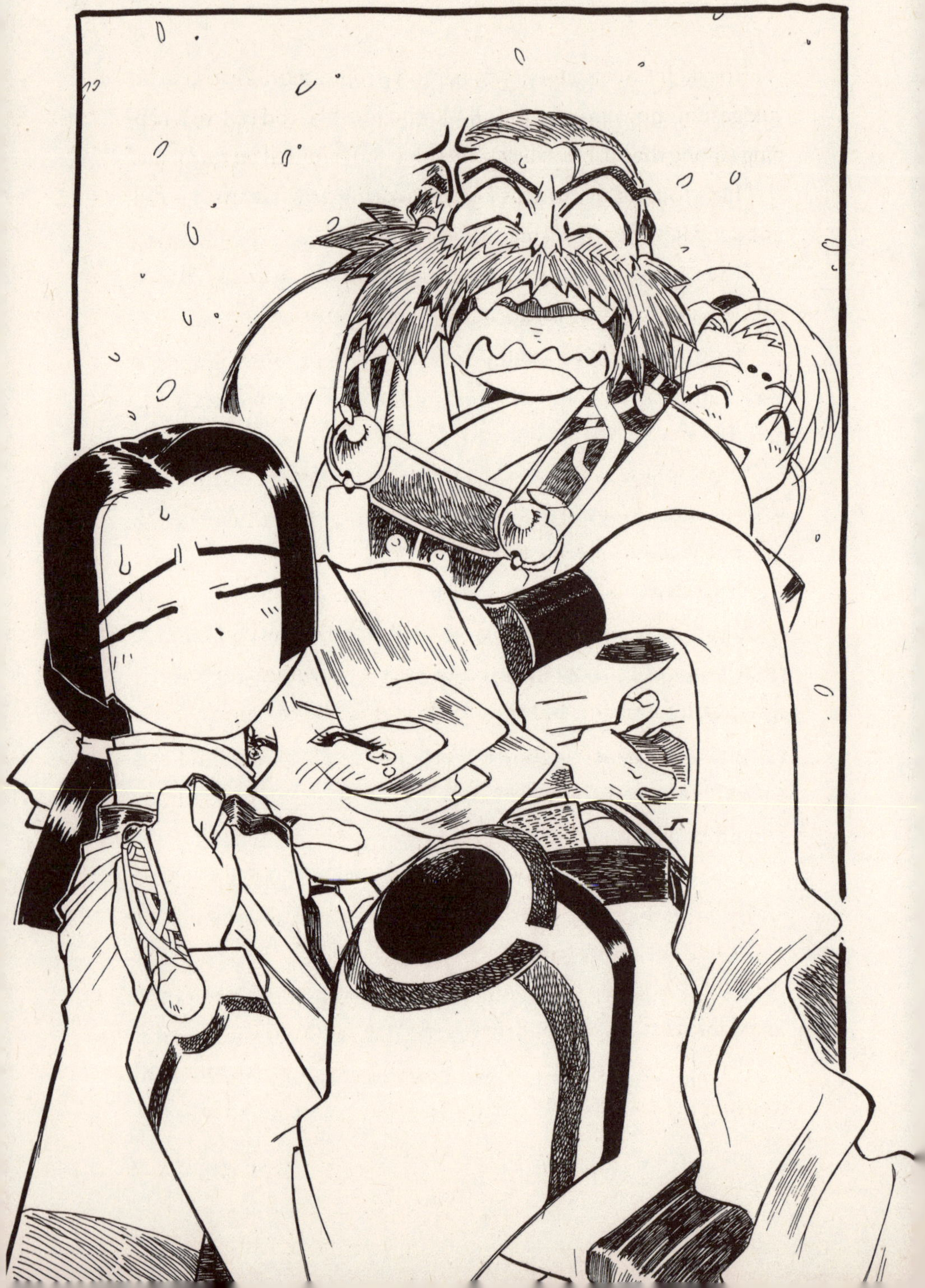

To add insult to injury, Seto admitted, blushing, "That day, the yukigasumi flowers were in full bloom, just like today. I was napping among the bushes, when something suddenly fell on top of me."

"He's too young for this!!" Considering how Utsutsumi did not deny it, this part seemed to be true.

"I resisted with all my strength. But I was too weak…" Seto dabbed her tears with the hem of Yosho's clothes.

"How are you weak, you old bag?!" Nobody could deny this point.

"And he reached for my heaving bosom…"

"No! I tripped! And I fell on top of you; that was it!!" Unable to hold back, Utsutsumi shouted.

"But you touched my breast."

"It was an accident. I didn't *mean* to. I fell on top of you, so I couldn't help it! The teacher told me to go look for you because you didn't show up, even though the entrance ceremony was starting already! And you were napping like you didn't have a care in the world… Besides, I was only nine years old at the time!!" He did not realize that he was telling the whole story himself.

"Mother was 4500 years old at the time, by the way." Misaki certainly did not know when to keep quiet. Sure enough, she got a knock on the head from Seto.

"That was not necessary!"

"Ow…" Misaki glared at her reproachfully, though it was commendable that she'd kept her hold on Utsutsumi.

"I was so surprised… It had been so long since anyone had touched my bosom." The terrifying scowl transformed into the expression of a fragile victim; her face blushing, Seto leaned coquettishly against Yosho. Since she was breathtakingly beautiful, the whole thing seemed sensual upon first glance. But after seeing the withering glare she'd aimed at Misaki, not even the most hot-blooded man would be turned on.

"Well, of course. Nobody would be reckless enough to harass the demon princess of Jurai." Utsutsumi thoughtlessly let slip out what Yosho had kept to himself.

"Yosho-chan, Caterpillar Face is bullying me. After all he did to me!" Seto clung to Yosho, collapsing into tears.

"A boy of tender years simply tumbled on top of you, and you said, 'I've been ruined and can't get married anymore. You'll have to step up and take responsibility' in all seriousness..."

"I was joking."

"How was a nine-year-old boy supposed to know?! I could barely eat from sheer terror for a whole month..."

"You collapsed from malnutrition and went to the hospital, right?" Without missing a beat, Misaki made another dig at her father.

"That's right! And 130 years of suffering later, I finally got up the courage to face you, and I offered to take responsibility, and you..."

"What did she do...?" Yosho asked.

Seto stuck out her tongue. "I burst out laughing. He took 130 years, and he proposed without as much as a preface..."

"130 years is too short after learning your true nature!!"

Yosho remembered that the older generations were unanimous in calling her terrifying.

Seto nodded, satisfied, and turned to Yosho with a smile. "So there you have it. He tried to take you with a myriad of excuses because he was afraid I was going to talk about what he just detailed to you himself."

"Oh..." Yosho looked sidelong at Utsutsumi, who was aghast upon realizing what he had done.

"You told him everything, so there's nothing to worry about anymore, is there? Come along, Yosho-dono."

Yosho looked behind him as Seto led him away and saw Utsutsumi drowning in melancholy, his hands planted on the ground and his head hung low. For the first time, he realized why Azusa, his father, gave his full attention to how he handled Seto, why those who really knew her feared her so much, and why she was called the demon princess of Jurai. *I didn't want to understand like this... I'll be careful from now on, too,* he thought from the bottom of his heart.

"Welcome, Seto-sama, Misaki-sama, and Yosho-sama." Seto had brought Yosho to the Academy principal's room. He was an old man, but he was hale and hearty, and unlike others, he was unabashed when faced with Seto. Seto and Misaki, likewise, had casual expressions, without their social masks.

"I summoned the person you requested not long ago, so he should be here momentarily."

"I see. That's good timing... Were you watching us come over?" Seto turned with an embarrassed smile.

"Yes, I can see very well from the window here. I hoped you wouldn't bully Utsutsumi-dono so much. And Misaki-sama!"

"Yes, sir!!" Misaki straightened up nervously and stood at attention. It was rare for her to act like this with anyone besides Seto. Seto would later tell Yosho that the principal used to be Misaki's mentor back when she was in school.

"You should lay off on riding Seto-sama's coattails and engaging in wacky hijinks. You are a *mother* now."

"But, sir…"

"But what?"

"Nothing…" Her voice was barely audible. Yosho could imagine what her student years were like. Getting scolded like this often, probably.

"Now, Mr. Principal. That's probably enough, since Yosho-dono is here and all." It was embarrassing to be scolded in front of her son, even a stepson.

He agreed with what she had to say, but he looked at the flowers outside and said, "Seto-sama, were you rehashing that old story again?"

Seto hesitated for a moment but then feigned innocence with unconcerned laughter. If Utsutsumi had been here, it would have been awkward to say the least. The moment the principal opened his month to say something, there was a knock on the door.

"He's here. Come in."

"Excuse me!" Hirata Kanemitsu, with an Imperial Academy uniform, strode into the room. But as soon as he did, he froze upon seeing who was also present.

"I apologize for the sudden summons." The principal had

anticipated Kanemitsu's reaction, spoke to him gently to ease his anxiety, and placed a hand on his shoulder to reassure him.

"Um...what did you need me for?" Kanemitsu managed to speak somehow, but he was still nervous. It was little wonder, as he was facing Misaki, the wife of his sovereign, and though married, still the most popular among the warriors; and Seto, her mother, feared by friend and foe as the demon princess of Jurai, the legendary Amazon. For Kanemitsu, who idolized them, it was unreasonable to ask him not to be nervous.

Kanemitsu's demeanor resulted in showing Yosho the position he held as a member of the Imperial Family. A mere encounter petrified people, striking fear deep in their hearts. He also saw how immature he was compared to Seto's charisma. This meeting was a shock for Yosho as well.

"Don't be so nervous. We're here today as Yosho's family." Seto gently took Kanemitsu's hand without putting any weird pressure on, which was unusual for her. Although that was enough for his cheeks to flush and beads of sweat to appear on his forehead.

"Uh-oh!!" Yosho almost shouted as he glanced at Misaki. The corners of her mouth were twisted and trembling slightly. Misaki had the habit of glomming onto anything and anyone she deemed cute. She held back while she was on official business as Empress, but when she came close to her limit, this was the warning signal. *If she were to glom onto Kanemitsu-dono right now, he might die from shock.* But Yosho could not hold her back, and Seto was in the middle of introductions. His eyes met with those of the principal, standing a step behind Kanemitsu, and signaled him by glancing towards Misaki.

"Seto-sama...! Here, would you like to sit down on the sofa...?" As hoped, the principal was aware of Misaki's habits and deftly let Seto know of Misaki's situation.

"I'm sorry, I was being inconsiderate... Please." Seto stepped back to make way for Kanemitsu and did not forget to nonchalantly step on Misaki's foot.

"Ow!!"

Seto encouraged Kanemitsu to sit down, then sat across from him and cut to the chase. "We asked you to come here today to thank you for taking care of Yosho at Galaxy Academy, and also..." Kanemitsu clenched his fists tightly and looked down. He thought he was going to be rebuked for being Kasen's puppet as well as House Amaki's. With Yosho being there, he could not think of any other business. Seto noticed all this and continued with a smile, "Kanemitsu-dono, would you want to study at the Academy again?"

"What...? Galaxy Academy?!" Kanemitsu lifted his face at the unexpected words.

"Yes, that's right."

"Did Yosho...?!" He regained some of his composure, thought Yosho had said something to Seto, and turned to face him. Yosho shook his head, barely perceptively, denying it.

"It was truly unfortunate that you had to return during the exam period and were unable to take the exams in four subjects. However, I received a report that of the eleven subjects you were able to take the exams for, your grades were all at the top of the class. If you are willing, I shall permit it under my name, Kamiki Seto Jurai."

This offer was extremely appealing for him. And an imperial mandate from Seto herself. But Kanemitsu was unable to answer and remained silent for a while. Seto waited patiently. She knew why he hesitated, what he was particular about, and could predict how he would answer. Kanemitsu opened his mouth as if wringing the words out, "Um…I went to study there on orders from the Amaki Family. And I returned to Jurai upon those orders. Going to study at Galaxy Academy was my dream. I could never express enough appreciation for your kindness, but my desire is that this is one dream I must bring to fruition on my own…"

There were some things that could not be conferred, even by the Imperial Family or people he respected. Kanemitsu had ruined it once. He realized it was due to his own inexperience. He knew that he would not make the same mistake again. To work for Seto and Misaki, his idols, was what he wanted. But he could not as long as he could not be confident in himself. He could not honestly say that he wasn't resentful of the Amaki Family for forcing him to return to Jurai. He never wanted to have to resent Seto or Misaki because of his inexperience. He was yet another awkward, stubborn Jurai man.

"All right…" Seto answered regretfully, but inside, she was satisfied that he had answered exactly as she had expected. But there was no way Seto was backing down, and of course she had prepared her next scheme. "But Kanemitsu-dono, while applying to the Academy will be easier than before, you will still need to pay a substantial sum. It will take you decades to raise the funds."

"I am prepared for that…"

"Kanemitsu-dono, would you like to make a wager with me?" She turned a provoking smile to him. She was revealing her true colors.

"A wager…?"

"Yes. The rules are simple. I will provide, out of my own pocket, twice the amount Jurai's federally financed study would provide. We will divide the expenses necessary for study by the number of exams needed for minimum credits in both semesters. If you are top of the class in those exams, I'll pay the entire amount; if you are second, I will pay half; if you are third, half of that again; and so on every time you fall in rank. If you are the top in all your subjects, you will owe nothing for the entire year. I will provide bonuses for other exams you pass and awards you earn. You can devote yourself to study as long as you want, whether decades or hundreds of years. Meanwhile, I will not interfere with anything you do. Once you have had your fill, you will come work for me to pay off whatever you could not offset." With skillful intonations of her voice and expressions, and subtle pauses, she pulled him into her grasp. "What do you think? Would you accept?"

"Is that all?" The conditions seemed easy for Kanemitsu. In actuality, he had almost always been the top in the core requirements, so he was confident.

"But maintaining top ranks every single time is a difficult undertaking. You might end up working for me for the rest of your life. If you're not confident, you shouldn't do it. Well?" It was a gentle provocation for Seto. Of course, Kanemitsu had been so nervous just a minute ago, and now he was excitedly discussing a wager with Seto. She was good at making him play her game.

"All right! I accept!!"

"Then that's settled!"

Kanemitsu reflexively took the hand outstretched by Seto. "...!!" After the fact, he realized that he was holding her hand, blushed, and let go.

Seto chuckled, "Kanemitsu-dono, when will you start? You can go right away, but what does the principal think?"

"Kanemitsu-kun, what are your thoughts?" The principal's tone was a little flabbergasted.

"I-I'd like to go after the training voyage..."

"Yes, that sounds good. Seto-sama?"

"All right, I shall make arrangements. I will say this again during the ceremony, but please have a safe voyage. I will await your return."

"Have a nice trip."

Kanemitsu blushed even further at Seto and Misaki's kind words. The students attending the ceremony were looking forward to these words. The words normally saved for millions of citizens were shared among a few select hundred. But these words right now were for Kanemitsu alone.

Yosho thought of another gift. "This will be Kanemitsu-dono's first long voyage."

"That's right...then here is something from me." Since Seto

had started this custom herself, the words from Yosho clued her in. She cut off a lock of her hair and handed it to him.

"Th-th-thank you!!" Kanemitsu was touched and moved to tears.

"Oh, a good luck charm? Then I will also." Misaki grabbed her ponytail, and...

"...!!" Everyone present opened their eyes wide in shock. Misaki chopped off a full third of her long hair and handed the bundle over with a smile. Kanemitsu, overcome by nervousness and extreme emotions, lost consciousness where he stood.

"Seto-sama, thank you for Kanemitsu-dono." After Kanemitsu had left the room as if walking in a dream, Yosho bowed deeply to thank Seto.

"Talented youth is the most valued treasure in Jurai. This was the obvious thing to do." Seto looked at Yosho with her best smile. However...

"This will be the best day of Kanemitsu-kun's life. I pray that he will never turn wise to your machinations." The principal's words were genial but barbed.

"Did I overstep my bounds?"

"Not at all. I'm just saying I hope he won't discover you had the Academy's invitation to him as a scholarship student shelved."

"What?!" Yosho looked at Seto in shock.

"Oh, you knew? I didn't want anyone else to have him. This is our secret, Yosho-dono," Seto chuckled.

Yosho was speechless. A scholarship would have been fully paid for by the Academy, and the student would not have to pay it back. This is the point at which his father the Emperor of Jurai would have said... "Old bag." Though, rationally speaking, this was very much in line with the way she was. At least Kanemitsu would not be unhappy. Seto was one of the best to call one's master, despite a few parts of her disposition, and he respected her. He would never be bored being at her mercy. "I can't believe her..."

There was a god and a demon on Jurai. Yosho remembered the words of the leader of the pirate guild when they sought asylum from the Galaxy Police.

Airi Again

Yosho completed his public duties on Jurai for six months and returned to the Galaxy Academy.

"Welcome home, Yosho-kun." Just like a year ago, Airi Magma was waving in the lobby of the deserted space port lobby.

Yosho, seeing her unchanged, remembered when he first arrived at the Academy. They exchanged greetings. "It's been a while, Airi-dono. I'm glad to see you're looking well." He respectfully bowed, but when he raised his head, Airi stared at him sullenly. "What's the matter…?" Without a word, Airi bonked him on the head. "Ow! Wh-why would you hit me?!"

"No reason. How is Funaho-chan?" Ignoring his stunned reaction, Airi walked onto his ship. Her straightforward way of directing her inner anger at others was unchanged.

Oh brother… Only after Airi-dono hits me does it truly feel like I've returned to the Galaxy Academy. Yosho smiled wryly and followed Airi as she stormed off.

As soon as she stepped onto the bridge, Airi let out a shriek of delight and a shiver of joy. A mass of Funaho puppies stormed towards her. "Funaho-chan, how *are* you?" She leapt into the wave of puppies, expressing her joy with her whole body. After a while, her face emerged from the puppies. "Oh, you have a lot of paperwork. You should go get that done."

"And Airi-dono, you are…" He was about to ask what she was going to do but stopped. It seemed obvious. "Then I'll get going. Funaho, take care of Airi-dono."

"See you later!" The sight of Airi and several hundred puppies all staring at him was quite a spectacle. After Yosho left the bridge, Airi sighed, looking at the puppies. "Funaho…your friend has come back, reverting to the same face he had when we first met," she mumbled sadly.

She had been in the same boat. Bearing the heavy responsibility of being the eldest daughter of Gaira Magma, the leader of the head temple of Airain, she couldn't laugh wholeheartedly back then. She feared and felt contempt for the people of other sects. Her heart shackled, she had lost freedom of thought and vision, and it was the Academy that smashed that cage.

Airi wanted to show Yosho, who was very much like she was when she first arrived here, what it was like to laugh wholeheartedly. But even with the passage of several years, she could not achieve this. She would loosen up his heart (by knocking sense into him), but just as he started to smile candidly, he would go back home for six months. And life on Jurai, through those six months, took his smile away from him. Every time she saw him repeat this process, Airi experienced joy and then dejection.

Eventually she grew to feel strongly that Yosho should not go back to Jurai...

A month had passed after he left for Jurai yet again when Airi received a transmission. She opened her eyes wide upon learning the location of its origin. It was from Airai, her home.

She quickly changed out of the Juraian raw silk clothes she had bought from Yosho and stood in front of the display. The display showed a person seated on a gilded, ornate vermilion chair, wearing Airai holy robes, smiling feebly.

"I'm glad you look well."

"Father...?!" The transmission was from her father, Gaira. She saw his weak smile and winced, fearing that he had lost weight again. She quickly realized that he was at the council chambers and straightened up again. "How are you, Father?"

"I'd like to say so-so."

"Please take care of yourself..."

"Airi, I'm sorry... I..." Gaira mumbled feebly, and averted his eyes.

The jig was up, she thought. Her actions that defied doctrine were a problem at the Airai council. If her father had not protected her, acceding to her wishes to stay at the Academy, she would have been sent home a long time ago. But pressured by the council, he could no longer protect her.

She quietly bowed her head, sensing his kindness. "It's all right, Father. I'm grateful that you forgave my behavior for so long."

"That's quite commendable of you, Airi Magma." The screen switched to show Gorba, the deputy and leader of the largest faction, and the top-ranked member of the council by a significant margin. "In the council's name, I order Airi Magma's return! In two months."

"Two months! But I'll receive my diploma in six months," Airi appealed to the monitor in protest. Yosho would return to the Galaxy Academy in five months. She hoped that she would at least be able to say a proper goodbye. "Please, at least that…"

"Hmph, we've all had enough of your self-indulgence. Your conduct where you have forgotten your position as daughter of the Airai leader cannot be forgiven, no matter your bloodline! Isn't that right, Gaira Magma-dono?" Gorba scowled at Gaira as if he were glaring at a defeated party. Gaira's head hung low.

Gaira looked away but saw his daughter's pleading face and mumbled, "Airi…your mother was your age when she came to marry me."

His words indicated that there was an offer of an arranged marriage. She had suspected the moment Gorba gave the order for her to return. But more than surprise, it hurt Airi more to look at her father's lamenting face. "Who is the intended…?"

"That will remain secret until the marriage. But it is undoubtedly a good arrangement. You'll like him, Airi-dono. I guarantee it." In a complete reversal from before, Gorba was in good spirits.

"I understand…" They exchanged a few words, and with a smile, she cut off the transmission. She stood there for a while. Someone in Airi's position did not have the freedom of marriage.

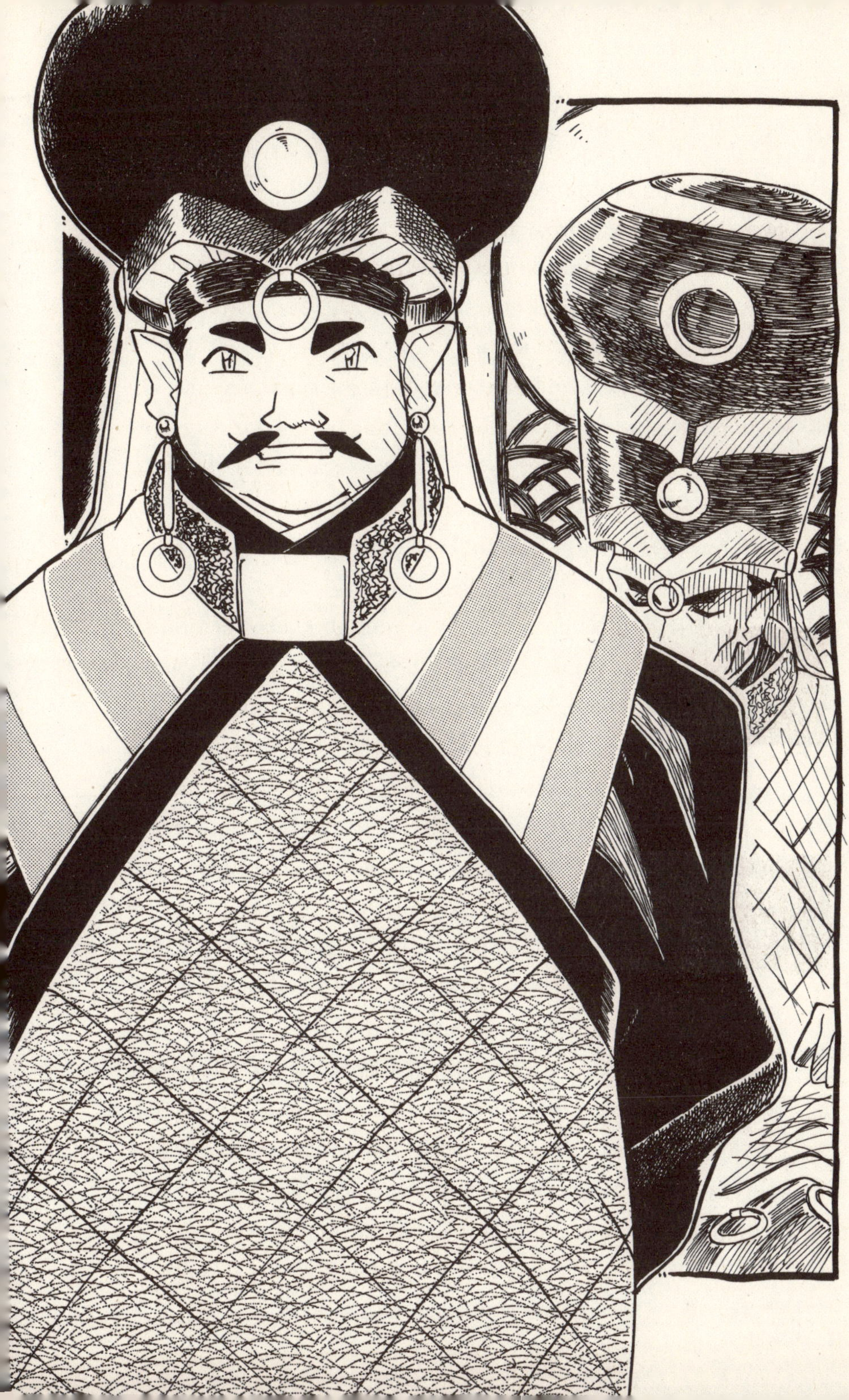

As long as she could not abandon Airai and her father, she had no choice but to accept her return and the marriage. Now that she had resigned herself to everything, her only regret was Yosho, whom she cared about like a real brother. Just as she had felt freedom at the Academy, she wanted to give him the same chances to be a child that she could have here. But his return to Jurai every six months took even that away.

If only he could stay here until graduation... Her wish would not be realized. Yosho's guardian was the Emperor of Jurai. No matter what she tried, she would not even be able to talk to him, let alone see him.

In those days of agony, there was some good news. The news that Kamiki Seto Jurai, renowned throughout the entire galaxy, let alone Jurai, was coming to visit the Galaxy Academy.

I've heard from Yosho-kun that not even the Emperor of Jurai was a match for Seto-sama. Maybe...

Airi immediately volunteered to be Seto's guide, but current diplomatic relations between Airai and Jurai were not great, and she did not get permission no matter how many times she inquired. Unlike Yosho, who came to the Academy as a student, Seto was visiting as a member of the Imperial Family of Jurai. The Galaxy Academy would obviously not allow it.

That did not mean Airi was going to give up. Even if the connecting threads were short and thin, she would not give up while there was still hope. A little leak could sink a great ship. She was following what she had been taught at the Academy.

It meant she was going after Kanemitsu.

"Yoo-hoo!" He turned heel at the genial greeting and promptly tried to get away, but Airi seized him by his neck. "Hey, why are you running away?!"

"Because I know what you're going to say!!"

"Then do it."

"Knock it off. How many times do I have to tell you, you can't see Seto-sama!!"

"It doesn't matter because I won't listen!"

"I'm just a warrior...on the lowest rung..."

"But you're going to be her guide, aren't you?!" Airi was not going to back down.

"Seto-sama isn't my friend. I'm not in a position to say anything personal! Asking your dad would probably work better than asking me."

"Don't be unreasonable!"

"*You're* unreasonable!!"

This dispute, unable to reach a consensus, always came to an end with Kanemitsu making an escape. A few days later, Airi was sprawled in bed in her room, dejected, staring at a TV special of Seto's welcoming reception. She'd used every contact she could think of but hadn't been granted an audience with Seto. However, when Seto's schedule was displayed on screen, she noticed a possibility and leapt out of bed.

"Right here... I could see her!" Airi was confident, watching Seto quietly smiling on screen.

Among the Imperial Family of Jurai, the biggest territory in the universe, Seto was the top in ability and popularity. Her visit was more elaborate than expected, and accordingly, security was on high alert. Since it was known that Airi had been scheming to meet with Seto, surveillance was harsh. Airi could not even see Seto from afar, let alone get close to her.

The facilities for the philosophy department, including the Washu Memorial Hall, were the only possibilities where she could run into Seto. Airi was friends with the old philosopher working there and had a pass to the private passageways. It was easy for her to sneak in, evading the monitors keeping an eye out for her. She decided to try when Seto finished touring the gallery, and the reporters and spokespeople had left. It would be a grave understatement to call it a mere international incident if Airi was shown meeting Seto on live broadcast.

Seto was supposed to meet privately with the philosophers after the tour. She should have only a few guards. At a corner of the building, Airi changed into the raw silk outfit given to her by Yosho on her birthday (which could be used as formal dress in the Imperial Family) and headed towards the passage she expected Seto to take.

As expected, the bodyguards on duty only stared dumbfounded at Airi wearing Jurai Imperial clothes. Airi was the daughter of a state leader, after all. The only one who seemed amused by the situation was the old philosopher standing next to Seto.

Airi walked up to Seto and kneeled down. "Pleasure to make your acquaintance. My name is Airi Magma; I served as guide for Masaki Yosho Jurai-sama. I understand I risk seeming rude in confronting you like this, but I wished to speak with you..." Her words trailed off. When she raised her face and looked at Seto's eyes, the tremendous pressure from them paralyzed her.

Without altering her gentle expression, Seto gracefully knelt in the same way. It was Airi's choice to kneel, but Seto determined that it would be bad optics for her to talk while looking down upon her. "Airi-dono, it's extremely unfortunate that your country and Jurai are currently in a difficult situation. It would not be prudent for the daughter of the Airai head of state to speak with me in public like this. All of us on Jurai are deeply grateful for what you have done for Yosho-dono. I sincerely hope that diplomatic relations will improve and we will be able to meet in an official function. Excuse me." With these brief words, she stood up and looked at the philosopher.

"This way." As if nothing had happened, the old philosopher led Seto to a back room, and the dumbfounded guards also ignored Airi and followed them.

Tears flowing down cheeks flushed with embarrassment and mortification, Airi was wracked with sobs. More than being shown the difference in their stature, her heart was full of the feeling that she would never be able to see Yosho again. Airi fled the building.

"That was the demon princess of Jurai that I've heard so much about?" the old philosopher said theatrically as soon as they entered the room.

"You're being rather suggestive. Is she one of your favorites?"

"Ha ha! Galaxy Academy students these days aren't as interesting. Few of them would dare pull off a stunt like that… It's unfortunate she lost. Well, she's a bit wet behind the ears to be fighting over a man with you…or, shall I say, inexperienced."

"Heh heh… Ha ha ha ha!!" Seto had desperately been trying to suppress laughter and could no longer hold back. "Did it seem that way to you, too? I thought so… It was so hard to keep from bursting out laughing."

"Ha ha ha. Truly unfortunate. It would've been more fun if only Washu-sensei and Naja-sensei were here… Though I suppose it would be a nuisance to others." Belying his words, the old philosopher spoke with delight.

"I hear you were their pupil. What were they like?"

"Oh, they toyed with us constantly. You knew it was trouble when they tacked a '-chan' on to your name. And they knew very well they were doing it. When they called you that, you ran out of there, fast."

"They were toying with you from there?"

"Oh, they went on the chase with delight. You didn't know what they were going to do to you when they caught you, so we would do whatever we could to escape. But Washu-sensei and Naja-sensei knew all our tricks. The record was six hours, thirty-one minutes, and twelve seconds. We usually got caught within the hour."

"Sounds like we'd get along…" Seto laughed with mixed feelings, knowing she had done similar things to Azusa and Yosho.

"Ha ha, I agree. Oh, can you guess how the record was made?"

"Whether they were highly skilled, or... They do often say, it's hardest to see what's under your own nose." Seto offered a likely answer from her own past experiences.

"Exactly! He had received the summons in his room and simply passed out from fear and anxiety." Their laughter echoed in the room, but the old philosopher gradually grew glum and mumbled, "Naja-sensei passed away, and Washu-sensei is missing. Since they've been gone, the Galaxy Academy has grown bigger, with more people...but it's also lonelier."

Seto, looking at him, grew sad, and mumbled more to herself than others, "The fun never lasts forever..."

Seto and Airi

AIRI RETURNED TO HER OWN ROOM from the Washu Memorial Hall and had flung herself in bed with her head facing the window. Night had fallen, and the nightly celebration was taking place here and there. She did not feel like taking part just now. "Yosho...kun..." At that moment, her stomach grumbled to protest its emptiness.

"You get hungry even now... Argh, enough!!" She leapt up, slapping her cheeks. Being lost in thought to the tune of a rumbling stomach, no matter how starry-eyed the dilemma, was stupid from an objective standpoint.

Just then, the doorbell rang. "Who is it?" Airi absentmindedly opened the door, thinking someone had come to take her to the celebration. The person she saw standing there left her speechless. It was Kamiki Seto Jurai.

"Good evening. May I come in?" Airi was too stunned to reply. "May I come in?"

The repeated question jolted her back to her senses, and she quickly ushered Seto inside, looking up and down the hallway to see if anyone had been watching.

"It's all right. Nobody saw me," Seto said, reading Airi's concerns.

"Seto-sama, what would happen if someone saw? It would not be prudent."

"Are you getting back at me? It's fine, I'm having dinner with the directors and the chairman." She turned the same gentle eyes towards her, but there was no trace of the pressure she had felt earlier.

"A complete turnaround..." Due to her position, she had seen people with plenty of charisma, but she had never seen someone with such extreme control. Airi knew she was called "the demon princess of Jurai," but she realized its true meaning when she saw this difference for the first time. She also realized that Seto had been teasing her when they met at the philosophy department...

"Whatever may I do for you?" she said a little grumpily and set up a shield to prevent sound leakage.

"You wanted to talk to me, right? And I thought I could have dinner with you." Seto showed Airi the two large baskets she was carrying.

The timing was so perfect that Airi blushed from embarrassment, thinking... no, *knowing* that Seto knew she had just been famished. She regained her composure and noticed that the dishes she was taking out of her baskets were those served at Narsis. "Seto-sama...aren't these..."

"The philosopher took me there for lunch. He said it's your favorite place to eat."

"You went there, Seto-sama?!" She stared at Seto in surprise. This was not flattering for Narsis, but she did not think it was a place to take a visiting royal.

"It was so good, so I had them make a basket." Seto was positively merry when it came to matters of food.

The proprietor must've been so shocked. Airi helped place the food on the table, and noticed several dishes she was not familiar with. "Seto-sama, it looks like there are dishes I've never seen at Narsis. Did you get them somewhere else?"

"I made that."

"What?!"

Seto had cooked it herself in the kitchen at Narsis. "They had distinctive and interesting spices available, so I wanted to try using them. These are based on Juraian cuisine, but the seasoning is by Narsis."

"You cook, Seto-sama?!"

"Is that so surprising?"

"It is..." She paused to think, but she had no other reply.

"Ha ha ha! I like your honesty!!"

"I apologize." Airi blushed in spite of herself but faced with Seto's frank and unguarded laughter, burst out laughing herself. They laughed together as if all that pressure had never existed. Airi's suspicion towards Seto melted altogether. It was all because Seto was the way she was.

Prompted by Seto, Airi took a bite of the food Seto had made, and she moaned, "It's delicious. Wow, it's really good." It was a taste she was used to, since it used a sauce from Narsis, but the different

Juraian style was pleasantly inserted, providing a fresh perspective.

"I'm glad you like it."

"I'm surprised she let you in the kitchen like that. She's very strict, and she'd never let anyone in if she hadn't eaten their food to her satisfaction before, let alone let them touch her implements... But with these skills, it makes sense."

"I brought ingredients I selected myself. I showed them to her, and she let me in," Seto said as if it was no big deal.

"That's all?"

"Yes, that was enough." Seto smiled at an uncomprehending Airi. "Airi-dono, do you cook?"

"What? No... I like to focus on the eating half..."

"I heard you have a keen sense of taste. She said you can discern the minute day-to-day differences that only she knows. She said she'd like to teach you things, if you're interested."

"I'd like to learn, if I didn't have my other job already..."

"Why don't you try, even if it's a little inconvenient? If you can make good food, you can survive anywhere."

"Yes, maybe I will."

"It must be nice... I taught my daughter the minimum, but all she wants to do is fill her stomach. Funaho-dono is too good a student, and there's nothing more I could teach... Ayeka-chan is a curiously clumsy cook, and she seems to prefer sewing."

"Oh..."

"If my next grandchild is a girl, I'm thinking about teaching her everything." They ate everything on the table while they chatted idly.

"Thank you for the meal. It was delicious."

"I'm glad you liked it. Would you like some dessert?" Seto brought out a massive cake from the basket.

"After all we ate...?" There was quite a volume of food. Even though Airi had stuffed her starving body, more than 70% of it had been eaten by Seto.

"You know how they say there's a separate stomach for sweets."

"I don't think I can..."

"Then how about some tea? It was grown in Mikagami. I brought water that was purified there, too."

This Airi accepted happily. Tea made from water purified by the Royal Trees was delicious, as she'd learned drinking on Funaho's bridge with Yosho. Feeling like herself again, she sighed and watched Seto happily portion out the large cake and genuinely enjoy it.

"I bet you could fit a little piece." Seto figured what she was thinking and placed a slice on a plate.

"All right, I'll have a little." Seto's cake, also homemade, was as delicious as expected. Full of fruit and nuts, Seto explained that it contained no sugar, highlighting only the flavors of the fruits.

"Jurai has the most diverse plant life in the galaxy, so there is a tremendous variety of fruit and nuts. There are countless variations of this cake depending on the combinations of fruit."

Airi nodded, impressed, completely in the palm of Seto's hand. She did not have the wherewithal to think while she was heady from the food and only remembered that she had something to talk about after she ate the last piece of cake and finished her tea.

"That was delicious. Thank you. I don't think I've had such a relaxing meal since Yosho-kun's... Oh!"

"Would you like another cup of tea?"

"Yes, please... I mean... No, I don't have time to be doing this!!"

"You're showing your true colors now," Seto chuckled, bemusedly watching Airi shout and stand up.

Airi glared at Seto...but seeing her smile made her lose her momentum.

"She said Yosho-dono looks like a child his age when he comes home from the Galaxy Academy."

"What?"

"Funaho-dono, Yosho-dono's mother, said sadly that he must be under so much stress on Jurai."

"Yosho-kun's mother?" Airi knew that Yosho's mother, Funaho, was in a difficult position on Jurai. And how much Yosho cared about her...

"Funaho-dono is very grateful to you."

Airi shook her head and mumbled, "I-I was shocked when he came back from Jurai and had this severe expression beyond his years. Right when he'd finally begun to act like a kid again, he reverted right back when he returned to Jurai... I wanted to ask you to let Yosho-kun stay at the Academy for good. Or at least..."

"At least what?"

"At least until he grows up a little more. I wanted him to have memories a childhood needs."

"Are you in love with Yosho-dono?"

"...!!" Seto's words were abrupt and devastating. Airi had not realized... or she was unconsciously trying not to realize. She felt Seto's eyes on her, and uncomfortably looked around. She did not know how to answer. She knew what the answer was but did not want to put it to words. She hated Seto for staring at her silently.

How could she ask this of me...? Various excuses came and went in her mind. But she felt that Seto would see through any lie.

"That's something I must not admit." She finally squeezed out those words, but then something snapped inside her, and she started yelling as if a dam had burst. "How could you ask me if I loved Yosho-kun?! You know that I can't do anything about it even if I did. If you had stayed silent, I wouldn't have had to confront it... In one month, I go back to Airai and that will be the end of it. Why are you making me face it now?!" Airi panted.

Seto quietly watched her, then said, "You're getting married when you get home?"

Airi's eyes opened wide. "If you know all this, then why?!"

"House Masaki always ends up being sacrificed for Jurai's sake. They have difficult romances." Seto's expression was so twisted with grief that Airi was taken aback.

"What?"

"Yosho-dono's grandmother and her brother, his father, and those who came before him... Jurai was built upon the sacrifices of House Masaki."

"I've heard of that. And that's why the Masaki House has the least power among the Four Imperial Houses."

"Heh, but that's a mistake."

"What do you mean...?"

"The people in House Masaki never choose Jurai. They don't love us. That's why the other houses hate them so much and love them even more... I love Yosho-dono's father."

"The Juraian emperor?! But..." She was about to say that Seto was married but hesitated. Seeing the seriousness in her eyes, it could not be said aloud.

Seto smiled self-deprecatingly. "Of course, I love my husband... But in some way, I love Azusa-chan even more. Ever since I went to bring him to Jurai, I've been watching him...raising him. I love everything that he loves. I won't let anyone or anything hurt him. Even if it was god incarnate..."

Airi's heart beat out of her chest, and her body froze. Seto's powerful emotions permeated the room so thickly they could be cut with a knife.

"I think of Yosho-dono as my son. I don't want him to see you... But I also do. I wouldn't care if he ends up having to abandon his home, like Amame-chan, his grandmother, if that was what he decided for himself."

"Abandon his home...?" Airi asked back and realized. "Renounce our homes to be together? But..." Yosho could never abandon his home where his beloved mother lived. Just as she could not abandon Airai, where her father lived. "That...can't happen..."

"Yes, I don't want that to happen. Yosho-dono is engaged to my granddaughter."

"I don't know what you're trying to say, Seto-sama. It's like you're just trying to confuse me..."

"Airi-dono, please tell me who you're betrothed to," Seto murmured, ignoring her question.

"I haven't been told…"

"You should know. Keila Magma-dono told you."

"…!!" This conversation with Seto was a succession of surprises. Just like most religions, there were bans on sexual relations for clergy. Keila was a leader of nuns and had authority equal to Gorba's. Airi officially belonged to a convent, and even Gorba or Gaira could not register her marriage without Keila's permission. Even if the council tried to keep the identity of the betrothed a private matter, they would have to tell Keila. And the nuns were far more moderate than the hard-liner priests.

"I have a pretty good idea who it is," Seto said. "But I need confirmation."

Airi had no idea how Seto agonized over saying those words. Or that those words…and simply the act of meeting Seto would change her fate.

"Why do you want to know?"

"Why does the council want to keep it a secret? The planning should be quite advanced by now. A marriage for someone like you should've been announced much sooner." Seto gave voice to questions that Airi had mulled over as well.

"Talking with foreigners about this, no matter what the council's intent may be…" Airi noticed even as she said those words that she was suspicious of the council. She sided with Airai over Seto, but she had no idea if that was really the right thing to do. That was how bewildered she felt.

Sensing her feelings, Seto continued, "You're well aware that Airai was more encouraging of missionary activities than other countries. And that Jurai has the freedom to practice any religion."

"But Airain…or other religions have not spread on Jurai. Jurai has the Royal Trees as their god."

"There were many religions at the time of Jurai's founding. We were a multicultural nation. But over the years, they settled on the Royal Trees as their god. But a lot of religious customs remain, along with the names of their gods. It's just that they all point to the Royal Trees."

Airi realized here that Seto knew that she wanted Tsunami, the progenitor.

Seto nodded as Airi turned towards her, "That's why a lot of people want to get a hold of a Royal Tree. Heh, most for military purposes."

Airi burst out laughing because "military" was a term far from the Funaho she knew.

"Heh, they don't like combat. And we don't want to make them fight, as much as we can. But Funaho, a First Generation Tree, can destroy an entire country on her own."

"How is that possible?!"

"Calculating back from the power of each generation, Tsunami is tremendously powerful. It would be easy to destroy the entire galaxy. A god indeed."

"What is Jurai trying to do with such power?" Airi felt fear toward the Royal Trees.

Seto shrugged, "Nothing. They're our friends, not our servants."

"Yosho-kun told me that the first Emperor of Jurai became friends with Tsunami."

"Yes. With that ring, you should be familiar with what they're like."

"Yes..." Hearing her words and remembering the Funaho puppies, the fear she just felt melted away. No matter how dangerous the weapons may be, there was nothing to fear with the knowledge that they would never be turned on people. "But..."

Seto continued in a frosty voice, "What would a Royal Tree do to someone who tried to coerce them?"

"Well..."

"How would you react, if it were you, Airi-dono?"

Airi was aghast. "I should've realized... If Tsunami-sama could destroy the universe, it would be simple for her to crush a country." The image of her home world being destroyed crossed her mind, and she shivered, understanding why Seto brought this up. "Does this have to do with my marriage?"

Seto nodded, "You know Amaki Kasen. It was the Imperial Amaki House who adopted him when he was an orphan. Nobody knows who his real parents are. But I bet we'll find out shortly after you get married."

"My betrothed is..."

"Have you heard of the Lufins?" Airi opened her eyes wide. She did not expect that name to come up. And Seto, seeing her reaction, knew she was right. "Kasen is supposed to marry the third daughter of the Imperial Amaki House. Then the Magmas and the Imperial Amaki House will be distant relatives."

No further explanation was necessary. Once a connection between the Magmas and the Imperial Amaki House was established, the Imperial Amaki House would support the missionary activities of Airain. And if a future Emperor came from the Imperial Amaki House…

"Marriage with people outside Jurai is difficult. But there are no rules for marriages within the clan. That's what they took advantage of."

Once externally substantiated, it became an internal matter. Seto could crush Kasen's marriage. But she could do nothing about Airi's problem. Now that she knew the truth, the umpteenth tear of the day ran down Airi's cheek. She mumbled, "They're so foolish. No, I feel sorry for them. They don't realize that they're locked in a cage called Airain. They even treat God like an object…"

The foolishness of trying to take hold of God, Tsunami, through force was pitiful.

But that council was going to decide Airai's fate. Airi was smart and could imagine her future. If Seto ruined Kasen's marriage, Airi's marriage would lose its meaning. It was her wedding that had value to the council. If she were simply the daughter of an authority figure, she would no longer be useful. But since she was descended from the holy leader, the only path remaining to her was to be a puppet just like her father.

The council knew that Airi made contact with Seto at the Washu Memorial Hall. They might not know about this meeting, but they would cast suspicions that Airi leaked the information.

She would be confined, only brought out to deliver a prepared performance when needed, or used for some other purpose… In any case, her life would not be a happy one.

"Yosho-dono will come to the Academy in two weeks to file paperwork for the leave of absence." Seto's eyes, looking deeply into Airi's, were making an appeal. She was giving her a final chance. If they sought defection at the Academy, and planted the Royal Tree on land there, neither Jurai nor Airai could do anything about it. But both Yosho and Airi had precious things in their homes they could not leave behind.

"I can at least say a final goodbye," Airi smiled sadly.

"I met your father once, long ago. Your father is stronger than you may think."

"What?!"

"I've overstayed my welcome. I need to get going." Seto stood up, walked up to the door, and turned around. "You must decide for yourself. Oh, let me remind you that it's not too late to learn cooking at Narsis, Airi-dono." With her usual gentle smile, she left the room.

As soon as Seto was out of view, all the energy left Airi's body. She collapsed onto her bed and began to cry.

Two weeks later, when Yosho visited the Galaxy Academy, it was the beginning of spring. Airi Magma was waving her arm wildly at Yosho in the empty space port lobby.

"Welcome back, Yosho-kun." She spoke to him the way she always did.

"It's been a while, Airi-dono." Yosho was also the same as usual. As always, they headed to Funaho's bridge.

"How have you been, Funaho-chan?" At Airi's question, a herd of puppy Funahos swarmed her. "Ha ha ha!!" Among the stifling scent of tender grass, light, and the pile of boisterous puppies, Airi's laughter echoed.

"Hey, Funaho! Airi-dono, calm down." The puppies went wild at Airi's laughter. The more Airi was excited, the number of puppies increased, and the ruckus escalated. Looking on, Yosho heaved a sigh, as usual. "They're always like this…"

"Look at you, looking all prim! Get him, Funaho!!" Airi and several hundred, or now close to a thousand puppies, pounced onto Yosho, licking and tickling indiscriminately, and after chasing Yosho, everyone tumbled into the moat.

"Oh, brother…" Yosho sighed deeply while changing clothes.

Airi took offense and turned to him. "You dare sigh at me now? Get him, Funaho…"

"Wait just a minute!!" Yosho tried to stop her, but it was too late. They were swallowed by the wave of puppies.

"Oh…but first we should have lunch. I'm hungry." The puppies paused at her words. "Right, Yosho-kun?"

"Huh? Oh…yes, then let's go to the living quarters." Yosho slipped out from among the puppies and made his way down, tugged by Airi.

"Let's eat in my room today." Airi's house was built at the base of the giant tree in the center of the living quarters. There was a small lake at the base, and her house was five meters above it.

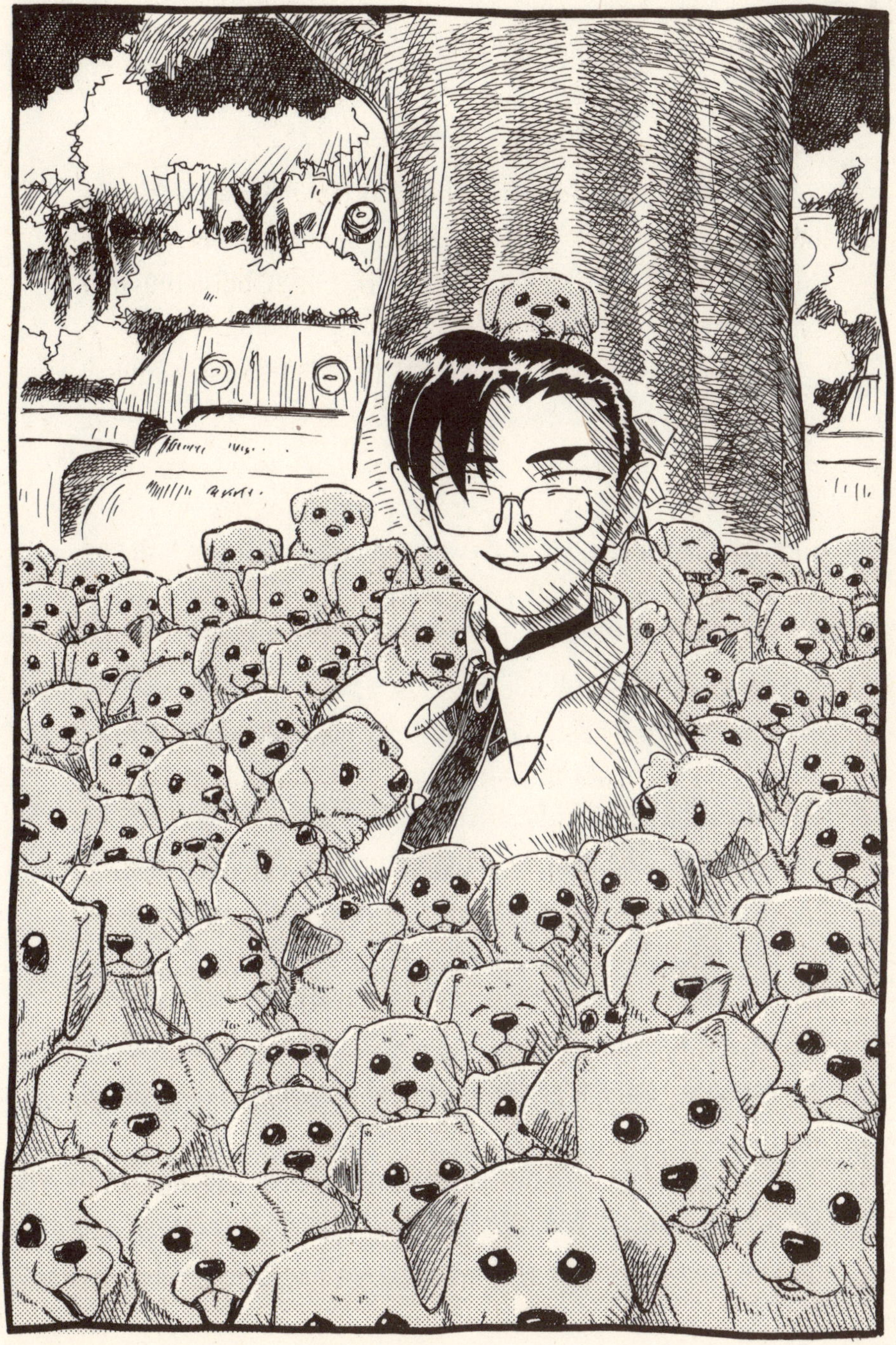

Yosho making Airi mad and getting slammed in there was becoming a bittersweet memory.

Airi entered the room, insisting upon making dinner, and entered the kitchen. Yosho knew of her skills at cooking and frowned, but while there was not much variety in the finished meal, it was quite delicious. But more surprising was the fact that it resembled the dishes at Narsis and also hinted faintly at Juraian cuisine. Airi had received personal tutelage from the proprietor at Narsis for the past two weeks.

After they ate, Airi used her killer technique seven more times. Yosho ran away, and Airi and the puppies gave chase. Yosho and Airi's laughter was just as loud as the yelping of puppies.

"Get him, Funaho!"

"Hold on, calm down!!" They knew they could not abandon their homes. So they wanted to spend as much time together as possible, in the place they loved the most. The sky had turned red with the sunset. On a hill, surrounded by a dense sea of puppies, Yosho and Airi watched the sunset, snuggling close to each other. Until the sun set below the horizon, neither spoke one word.

The one who started crying first was Airi. She placed her head on his shoulder, gritted her teeth, and tried to stifle her sobs. Yosho also buried his face in her hair. They did not need words. They did not want to part. But they had reasons they could not stay together.

Airi looked up with her tear-stained face at Yosho. Her trembling lips formed the words, "I love you... Yosho."

She pressed her cheek against his face, like a cat showing her affections. Yosho moved with her, and their lips came closer. Out of consideration for them, there was not a single puppy around.

Among the silence of the night, the only sounds were of their breath and the rustling of grass.

The day Airi went home, Seto revealed the origins of Amaki Kasen on the Juraian home world. As a result, his marriage to Shuzan's daughter was canceled. Airi's betrothed, announced on Airai, was not someone from the Lufins as Seto had predicted, but Gorba himself. The council's plot had been foiled by Seto.
Right afterwards, calling it a "religious ceremony" prior to the nuptials of the state head's daughter, the planet Airai transferred its political center to a satellite city and closed itself off to the outside world under the pretense that this would only be for a few years. Suddenly, others were not privy to anything that was happening within Airai.
Yosho on Jurai, without exception, could not find out anything about Airi. Seto would not say anything about it. He was driven by the impulse to go see her immediately, but he was aware of the consequences of taking such actions. Their emotions spun with nowhere to go, their feelings for each other that would never entwine for now...

Five years passed.

Ryoko's Attack

THAT DAY, there were countless explosions due to combat in the skies over Jurai. Acts of hostilities on the Jurai home world, the most powerful single nation in the universe, had not occurred for almost two thousand years. Jurai may have gotten inattentive, but this was a startling incident. The emergency alert echoed in the command center, where people were furiously working to verify the sudden attack.

One of the operators, a warrior, stared at the data on his display monitor and reported in disbelief, "J-Jurai's absolute defense zone has been breached. In less than a minute, whatever this is will arrive on the surface."

"It had to be when the Emperor is absent! What fleet is this?!" Just then, static ran on the monitors. "What happened, did we get hit?!"

"The flagship is still intact! This must be due to a distortion in space-time from the energy wave when the enemy fleet passed through." As soon as the operator finished answering, communications recovered. "There's a powerful energy reading... No, that's not possible!!" The operator could not believe his own eyes but confirmed that it was real multiple times before turning to his commander. "Th-there's only one ship!"

"What?! Even if they picked a time when the First and Second Generation ships are away, a single ship breached the defense zone? How is that possible...?" Everyone shuddered. A single Third Generation ship could annihilate a fleet of thousands under the right conditions, so a single ship coming through was not only reckless but suicidal. And yet this ship had picked a fight with Jurai by herself. She had broken through the defense zone and was getting closer.

A pillar of light flashed in the sky, and the next moment, a deafening roar was heard, along with the appearance of a black crystalline ship positioned several hundred meters above the surface. In the next moment, a tremendous impact shook Tenju.

"They're storming the place!!"

"We have confirmation that it's Ryo-Ohki!!"

"Ryo-Ohki?! The Black Destruction?!" the startled commander cried out. Those outside the supreme council did not know that Ryo-Ohki fought on equal terms with Emperor Azusa's Kirito during his voyages. Still, her name was known throughout the galaxy.

"Meowwww!" The moment an animal cry could be heard from the ship, three intercepting squadrons along with a Fourth Generation Ship went up in balls of flame in rapid succession.

"A Fourth Generation ship, in one strike?!" They had no

choice but to believe it now. A foe that could threaten Jurai was before them, on the attack! The coming of the Black Destroyer bathed the skies over Jurai in a crimson glow.

While Ryo-Ohki was attacking Jurai, the main members of the Imperial Family were all on tours abroad, and thus the First and Second Generation ships were on official government business away from the home world. Among them, Yosho had finished his duties quickly and already begun his return voyage.
"The home world is under attack?!"

"Yes, the intruder is a known space pirate flying a single ship called Ryo-Ohki. She is currently engaged in battle with the planet's defenses."

"We'll get there in about five hours. Have them hold out until then." The reporting warrior gave a brief salute and disconnected. Yosho ordered Funaho to increase speed at once. "I can't believe it's a single ship. So her name is Ryo-Ohki..."

Yosho had heard of the rumors. A pirate ship that didn't belong to any guild but acted alone. She was called Black Destruction for her sheer demolition power, but that was only rumor. Her pattern was usually to hit isolated planets far from large civilizations, so accurate accounts were not available.

"Was it a fluke? No...Jurai's defense zone can't be breached by luck alone." Yosho did not know at the time that Ryo-Ohki had once surpassed the power of Kirito, his father's ship... He knew that Ryo-Ohki had recently been involved in the thefts of important cultural assets and kidnappings of intellectuals at various locations around the galaxy. From the fact that the enemy was heading towards Tenju, it was obvious that they were after the Royal Trees.

"Ryo-Ohki... I'll find out if all the rumors are true." It might have been his pirate blood, but Yosho felt a little elated.

A pillar of flame lit up the sky. With a backward glance at the three sinking Fourth Generation Jurai ships, Ryo-Ohki continued to attack, winding her way hither and thither. On the bridge, a woman smiled, arms folded in front of her chest. Wearing a red and black combat suit, with spiky, pale-emerald-green hair, golden almond-shaped eyes, and crimson jewels at the nape of her neck and both wrists... Ryoko sat, completely drunk on the high of combat and destruction.

"Heh heh. Ha ha ha ha!! Come at me. Or I'll steamroll over you!" Ryo-Ohki turned purposefully towards where several ships were clustered.

"How can this be? They may be Fourth Generation ships, but each has the power of a flagship from any other country. The whole lot of them banded together can't stop this?" Moaning in the command chair as Ryo-Ohki trampled everything in her path was Masaki Tatsua, acting commander while the Imperial Family was away. "You still haven't made contact with House Amaki or Shuzan-dono?"

"We keep hailing them, but communications seem to be blocked. I'm afraid Shuzan-dono is..."

"Don't speak another word!" Tatsua gritted his teeth with

chagrin. Shuzan was supposed to arrive back on Jurai a day before Yosho, so obviously, he should have been closer than him. But he could not even be contacted, let alone located.

"The primary defense line has been breached!" the operator screamed.

"We can't even alter her flight path, let alone stall her?"

Ryo-Ohki was advancing in a zigzag pattern. Tatsua knew that this was Ryo-Ohki enjoying herself, not because she needed to evade attacks from Jurai.

"The enemy has reached the secondary defense line!"

"Well then..." Tatsua left the lieutenant next to him in charge and exited the bridge. He was going to sally forth with his own Third Generation ship.

There were currently five Third Generation ships on Jurai. With them in front and a dozen or so Fourth Generation ships as support, he estimated that it would be possible to push out Ryo-Ohki back into space.

However, only three Third Generation ships showed up at the rendezvous point. Unbelievably, the two ships owned by the Imperial Amaki House rejected the plan under the pretext of defending Tenju.

"Defend?! What could they do with only two ships?!" Tatsua himself was reluctant to even say those words. Two Third Generation ships would absolutely trounce an ordinary enemy. But the reality he was faced with made him lose faith in that assumption. "If they pass the final defense line, we're through. Damn you Shuzan, must you be so against House Masaki...?!"

The unmoving Amaki Jurai ships were ordered to watch and not act by Shuzan. He was clearly underestimating the severity of the situation, to give such an order. But for someone who was not personally witnessing the events, it could not be helped.

There was another factor critical to this disaster, and that was the growing fear of Ryo-Ohki. Even without Shuzan's order, those onboard the two ships defending Tenju did not want to enter this battle. What they believed to be absolute, the power of the Royal ships, was being destroyed before their very eyes.

Ryo-Ohki headed towards Tenju, leaving only destruction in its wake. Tatsua was determined to stop Ryo-Ohki even if it killed him. A Third Generation ship was piloted by the Imperial Family. She was outfitted with a metal combat hull unit that was almost shameful to equip, considering the raw power the ship already had.

"Now's not the time to be concerned about that!" Tatsua was an excellent warrior trusted by Seto. He would not allow pride to take over. Adapting battle plans on the fly, he turned the two ships towards Ryo-Ohki, for the first phase.

Suddenly, a number of spheres of light danced wildly around Ryo-Ohki and momentarily neutralized her sensors, stopping her in her tracks.

"Hmph... Light Hawk Wings." Ryoko clicked her tongue. She knew about their existence from Kagato... or rather, from the battle with Azusa's Kirito. On either side of the panoramic view she had from the bridge, the three Light Hawk Wings deployed by the two ships twinkled. "This is nothing!" The moment she tried to break away at full throttle, an extraordinary amount of pressure bore down on Ryo-Ohki's hull. The other Third Generation ship and the Fourth Generation ships were attacking.

Tatsua saw from the bridge that Ryo-Ohki was being imperceptibly pushed back into the atmosphere and grew confident in their victory. "It's working!"

"Heh heh, what's this attack? This isn't even close to that one other ship before. Thinking this would stop her is ridiculous." Ryoko laughed mockingly from her bridge, glowing red from the light of the attack.

In that instant, Tatsua's ship began to distort. "How could that be?! Everyone fire at will, focus on Ryo-Ohki!" The Juraian ships attacked desperately, but Ryo-Ohki deflected them all. "How could they block Third and Fourth Generation ships so easily? This could only be done...with Light Hawk Wings."

At the same moment, the two Royal Trees pinning Ryo-Ohki down let out a scream, and were thrown off, succumbing to her overwhelming power.

Ryoko smirked, her arms crossed in front of her. "They're a waste of time. Come on, Ryo-Ohki!"

"Meoww!!" Ryo-Ohki's high-pitched cry resounded above the Jurai skies. Perhaps overwhelmed, the three Third Generations ships hesitated and stopped attacking.

"Why aren't you firing?!"

"We don't know. But the units are all functional!"

"What?!" Tatsua understood that the Trees had stopped their attacks on their own. "That's not possible. That could only be done by someone with a Third Generation Tree or higher!" An absolute denial went through his thoughts. The Royal Trees were the equivalent of gods in their minds. Jurai had become such a powerful nation through their power. "I won't believe it!! That would be the end of this country!" He could not accept that there could be something superior to the Royal Trees. The Imperial Ships must be absolute. Ryo-Ohki must be destroyed, even if it meant his sacrifice. "We have a Third Generation Tree. If we all perish here, that would mean Ryo-Ohki would be more powerful than the Third Generation!"

"Meowwww!!"

Tatsua's ship, hearing Ryo-Ohki's high-pitched cry, turned off its Light Hawk Wings. The ship was out of control, and the bridge shook.

"Tatsua-sama, we must abandon ship!"

"Why? Why is this happening?!" Tatsua's ship was engulfed in flames and fell out of the sky.

Ryo-Ohki's attack hit its target, and Tenju was illuminated in a red glow. A girl burst out of a room in House Masaki in a corner of the giant tree. Her dark purple hair was bunched in two ponytails. This elegant girl was Masaki Ayeka Jurai. She was supposed to have gone on a voyage with her father Azusa, but she had her Tree Selection Ceremony immediately beforehand and thus remained on Jurai with her little sister Sasami. As a nation that prospered because of the Trees, it was only natural that becoming a partner with a Tree would be prioritized over everything else.

RYOKO'S ATTACK

"What in the world is the defense force doing? I'm going to go out myself!" She strode down the hallway as her attendants tried to stop her.

"Ayeka-sama, please stop."

"My Ryu-oh is the only Second Generation ship on Jurai right now."

"But you formed a contract with Ryu-oh only recently. The adjustments to the outer hull unit aren't even finished yet."

"But I cannot leave that scoundrel to rampage as they please. That would be inexcusable. I wouldn't be able to face my brother or Father!!" Currently, Ryu-oh had only just had a hull attached to the core unit and had not even made her maiden voyage yet. Ayeka aggressively launched the ship, paying no heed to everyone trying to stop her.

Ryoko detected Ryu-oh's launch from a corner of Tenju on Ryo-Ohki's monitor and knew that this ship, that had destroyed the dock gates on her way out and upwards, was different from the others. "This energy reading is an order of magnitude above the others. Looks like I'll get to have some fun."

Even so, her fighting style did not change. She simply routed everything that got in her way.

Ayeka's Ryu-oh deployed Light Hawk Wings to deflect the energy blasts emitted from Ryo-Ohki. Ryu-oh tried to counter-attack, but the attacks veered widely away from Ryo-Ohki and dissipated into empty space. Ayeka did not have a key to assist in her synchronization with the Tree, and the ship had just finished being outfitted. Since the adjustments to synchronize the unit with the hull were not complete, Ryu-oh was unable to properly harness the power of the Tree.

"This is nothing!" Ayeka clicked her tongue and continued the battle but soon found herself focusing entirely on defense. Still, Ryu-oh stayed intact due to the power of the Light Hawk Wings wielded by a Second Generation tree and because Ryo-Ohki (meaning Ryoko) was deliberately toying with her prey.

"Come on now, what happened to your spirit?!" Ryoko had energy to spare, but Ryu-oh's attacks were clearly now weaker than her initial volley. She keenly felt the possibility of defeat if she let down her guard. Multiple energy cannons were fired from Ryo-Ohki, closing in on Ryu-oh. The Light Hawk Wings deflected them all, but one of the blasts made a direct hit on Ayeka's favorite garden on one of Tenju's branches.

"My favorite garden! How dare you, you pirate!!"

"Your favorite, is it? Ha ha!" Ryoko concentrated fire on the garden on purpose. The flowers and trees were immediately incinerated.

"S-stop it. All the time I spent there with Oniisama... Please stop!" She had played with her brother Yosho in that garden countless times. That place full of memories was mercilessly destroyed, and Ayeka, with tears in her eyes, ordered Ryu-oh to an all-out attack. She was going to use the Light Hawk Wings not as defense but as an attack. They contracted into one spot, aimed at Ryo-Ohki. "Die!"

The moment she shouted, the unit's power controls overloaded. The outer hull, unable to withstand the energy load, went out of control, firing energy blasts randomly into the vicinity.

The energy blasts rained down like a shower of flames, and one of them destroyed the branch holding Ayeka's favorite garden where it connected to the trunk! "Noo?!"

The gardens teetered and fell, accompanied by Ayeka's screams. A "branch" on Tenju was several thousand meters long, and the sight of its falling was awe-inspiring. An energy blast grazing past Ryo-Ohki violently shook her, even though all the focused fire of the Third Generation ships had failed to move her one inch.

"Ooh, scary. That's a princess of a pirate nation for you; when she flips out, watch out! Ryo-Ohki, you handle the rest." Ryoko watched the whole thing unfold with a wry smile. She disembarked and made her way inside Tenju through the gaping hole left by Ryu-oh. However, the Jurai warriors detected the intruder, and ten of them ran towards her at once.

"Wh-what's this?!" They stopped in disbelief. Behind Ryoko was an eerie, translucent specter with four red eyes, sharp claws, and fangs. As her name implied, Ryoko had the ability to summon evil spirits. But these were not summoned consciously; they had appeared, manifested by the excitement of combat.

Indifferent to the tumult outside, the door to the Hall of Royal Trees was quiet. The occasional vibrations from the blasts were the only indication of the fierce battle.

"Wow." Three-year-old Sasami looked up at the giant door

with eyes full of curiosity, oblivious to everything outside. The other day, she had seen her older sister Ayeka go inside and whined that she wanted to do the same, a request which was rejected by the grown-ups. She had snuck away, hiding from Mama, her nanny, who was nervous about Ryo-Ohki's attacks, and come here. She slowly reached for the doors that were too big for a child to open, and they parted before her on their own. It was as if it beckoned Sasami inside.

Once inside, Sasami squealed with delight upon seeing the countless crossing paths and the verdant Royal Trees dotted along the way. Spheres of light surged from the foliage like fireflies, and the Trees began to sing a gentle melody. Sasami was captivated with this magical sight, walked onward, looking around, and unknowingly passed through the doors of the transport. Indeed, Sasami was transported to the zone of the Second Generation Trees, to where she could only be taken if she were accepted by them. Sasami, enjoying herself and politely greeting each Tree, went further.

Meanwhile, outside Tenju were two Third Generation ships, Light Hawk Wings deployed, and one of the House Amaki ships that had been avoiding a skirmish with Ryo-Ohki. They were caught up in Ryu-oh's attack, still out of control. Damage was minimal, but the lost focus meant the Light Hawk Wings vanished. Ryo-Ohki took advantage, and one of the ships, pierced by an energy blast, made contact with Tenju's trunk, causing a large explosion.

This was where Fate intervened. When this larger jolt shook

RYOKO'S ATTACK

Tenju, Sasami slipped and fell into the abyss. It happened in a blink of an eye. With a scream, Sasami disappeared into the pitch-black darkness.

"Ayeka-sama, please stop the attacks. Tenju isn't going to last!!" Ryu-oh's bridge shook wildly, and Ayeka, collapsed on the floor, saw Tatsua on the screen with relief and confusion. His ship had sunk, but the Royal Tree had protected the core unit, and he and his crew were safe.

"Uncle Tatsua, I can't stop it! The hull unit has lost control..."

"Blast the hull off, hurry!!"

As she was told, Ayeka tried an explosive release of Ryu-oh's hull. But already overloaded, there was no outlet for its energy, and the whole thing exploded. With a close range blast, Ryu-oh was blinded, and the smoke allowed Ryo-Ohki to close in. Suddenly, Ayeka saw Ryo-Ohki fill her screen. She screamed. There was not even any time to deploy the Light Hawk Wings!

"Onisamaaaaa!!"

The moment Ryo-Ohki tried to attack, the ship was struck and repelled. A blink of an eye later, there was a deafening roar. Storming through the clouds was Yosho's Funaho. The Light Hawk Wings captured the shock wave generated by unmitigated entry into Jurai and redirected it right at Ryo-Ohki.

"Yosho-oniisama?!"

"Ayeka, get back!" he commanded and fired an energy blast towards Ryo-Ohki to keep her in check. He knew she would evade it, but it pushed her further away from Tenju.

Tatsua sent a transmission. "Yosho-sama, there's an intruder in Tenju!"

"So this is a decoy. I'll be right there!" The joy of reunion, remorse, everything would wait until later. He had to get this incident, unprecedented in the history of Jurai, under control – that was Yosho's job.

However, it was clear that if he tried to transport to Tenju from Funaho, Ryo-Ohki would notice and attack the transport coordinates. Yosho had no choice but to pull away from Ryo-Ohki and enter from the other side. "Funaho, I'm counting on you!" he shouted the moment he transported from the bridge. Funaho turned her bow towards the pursuing Ryo-Ohki and fired a volley of energy blasts. The battle of two ships without their masters shook and rattled Tenju.

Looking on, Tatsua breathed a sigh of relief. Funaho, the First Generation ship and one of the most powerful on Jurai, had come at last. Ayeka felt the same on Ryu-oh, but for her, the relief was not due to Funaho, but the fact that her beloved brother Yosho was here. He would never be defeated by a pirate. This, she was sure of from the bottom of her heart.

Ryoko entered Tenju, defeated the warriors one after another, and was about to reach the Hall of Royal Trees, which contained whatever it was she was looking for. "So that's the entrance!!" She fired off some energy blasts, but the door was unscathed. "How about this?!"

The moment she tried to increase the energy in the blasts, the three jewels in her wrists and neck shone bright, and she let out a bloodcurdling scream of agony. Pain on a level she had never felt racked her body. Even the punishments she received when she ignored Kagato's orders were not like this.

"What is this? What's going on?!" She clawed at her throat, glaring at the door, trying to endure the pain.

Beyond the door, in the deepest part of the Hall of Royal Trees, Sasami lay in the darkness of another dimension. It was clear that she had died instantly. A drop of her blood fell onto the surface of the purest water. In the center of this water was a small tree. It was not First or Second Generation. It was Tsunami's Tree, the Progenitor of Royal Trees.

"What are you doing… Tsunami…" Ryoko mumbled, half unconscious from the pain, the moment Sasami's blood dripped into the water,

"I'm keeping my promise… with my friend." Sasami's mouth moved imperceptibly. In the next instant, her body dissolved into beads of light and was absorbed into Tsunami. The tranquil water churned and swirled. Sasami and Tsunami's souls assimilated into a single entity, and a new body was reconstructed in the whirlpool. This dimension created by Tsunami was indeed a maternal womb.

Ryoko, completely in a trance, spoke without consciousness, "We shall meet again… Tsunami…"

As Ryoko blacked out, Yosho stood behind her. "You must be Ryoko. I am Yosho, Crown Prince of Jurai. This is no place for you! Leave at once, or else…"

He gave her an obligatory warning, and when she did not respond, he attacked with his sword. But Ryoko evaded it, still unconscious. Yosho noticed that her moves were unnatural and relented for a moment, when Ryoko, eyes still closed, slowly raised her arms into an attack stance. "Oh hell...!"

The energy blasts filled the hallway, and a tremendous blast assaulted Yosho. But the one blown outside Tenju was Ryoko. Falling, Ryoko finally came to. "What...? What... am I doing?"

"The Tsunami unit is out of our reach now."

"What did you say...?" Something spoke to her from within. The one inside her, who told her the shadow she saw when she fought Azusa, the Emperor of Jurai, was Tsunami... No, that would not be accurate. The voice came from the three jewels embedded in Ryoko. Sometimes she felt a consciousness within those three jewels.

"There is nothing I can do here now."

"What do you mean?"

"..."

"Dammit! Ryo-Ohki!!"

The flashes of light and explosions subsided, and Yosho, realizing that he was unhurt, ran to the opening just as Ryo-Ohki, having collected Ryoko, rose up towards the sky. "That was fast, but..." He called for Funaho at once. Ayeka ran in, having disembarked from Ryu-oh.

"Yosho-oniisama!"

"I'm going to go capture Ryoko." It was the last direct conversation they had. Yosho leapt into the air, and Funaho transported him to the bridge. He had her search for Ryo-Ohki and opened a channel to Tatsua, who had returned to the command center. "Tatsua-dono, the diplomatic order I received from the Emperor of Jurai was concluded as of 27.1.28.138 when I entered Jurai space."

"What are you saying? You mustn't—anything but that!"

"As Crown Prince of Jurai, I order you with First Generation Funaho."

"Please, no further!"

Ignoring Tatsua's heartrending pleas, Yosho continued, "With the completion of the Emperor's order, I, Yosho hereby order command on Jurai to transfer to me." Those words meant that Yosho would take full responsibility for the entire string of events after Ryoko invaded Jurai. Yosho cut off the channel, burst through the atmosphere, and flew off into space once again.

Tatsua might think that taking full responsibility may resolve the problem, but even if he died (and he would sacrifice himself for this), Shuzan would not stop pursuing House Masaki for liability. The current head of House Masaki was Yosho's mother Funaho, from the point that his father, Azusa, became Emperor of Jurai. Shuzan would seize onto this fact. But if the responsibility fell on the top candidate for the next Emperor of Jurai, it would be possible to direct his ire at Yosho alone. Of course, the line to the throne was meaningless for people who were only a couple decades apart in age, considering their lives spanned several thousands of years. But with Shuzan's abnormal obsessiveness, he was ecstatic to have even one person to blame.

But then, even if Yosho successfully captured or defeated

Ryoko, it would not solve the problem. Allowing a single ship, a mere lone pirate, to invade the home planet was that humiliating for Jurai.

"Well, if Ryoko and I were to die at each other's swords, Shuzan-dono would be on cloud nine and conduct a lavish state funeral with all expenses covered by House Amaki... Mutual destruction, huh..." Perhaps Yosho dying with Ryoko was the best solution. "Once I'm gone... Heh heh, hahaha..." Even though he was facing what could be a fatal battle, he could not help but laugh. It was not from fear. He was enjoying this. He felt he was going to finally experience true freedom.

"Liberated...? What am I thinking? Do I desire death?" Looking back, he had been bound to Jurai due to Funaho. But now he would be liberated to benefit Funaho.

It wasn't that he had suffered in his life so, but the eyes young Ayeka had turned to him weighed heavy. It was a cliché, but she was in love with the *idea* of love. Those eyes held not passion but a desire for sanctuary. She had not realized this, but even now, they had not changed. Whenever Ayeka spoke of marriage, it stabbed Yosho's heart. It was all he could do to simply nod.

"Poor Ayeka..." Yosho repeated what Airi had said years ago. Airi had given him peace from his feelings for Misaki. But Ayeka would not be able to give him peace from his feelings for Airi. No matter how much he loved her, Ayeka was a little sister to him. And ironically, Ayeka herself was making it worse.

While he indulged in ruminations, he was hailed by Kirito. It was Azusa. "Yosho!"

RYOKO'S ATTACK

"Father."

Azusa stared blankly at Yosho. He had accepted everything he had done. "I received the report. I know you will be successful in your hunt of the intruder."

Yosho bowed deeply and accepted his orders. "I will bring back the space pirate Ryoko's head!"

The battle data sent from Tatsua back on the home world to Funaho held terrifying facts about Ryoko. Initially, Jurai's main computer detected three energy clusters within Ryo-Ohki, which were thought to be her reactor. But once she approached Tenju, the reactor was gone...or rather, it had moved off of Ryo-Ohki. That mobile reactor was Ryoko. An unimaginable amount of energy was being generated from locations on her wrists and neck. Yosho furrowed his brows.

"*That's* the source of the power that overwhelmed even a First Generation ship?" No matter who Ryoko was, this was way beyond the kind of energy any one individual could possess. He looked over at Funaho tracking Ryo-Ohki, who was on a course into deep space, exiting the galaxy. Yosho paused to ponder.

"Come to think of it...there's an asteroid belt relatively close to here, full of rare metals and a gigantic hyperspace transport device that warps them to Jurai. It uses a Third Generation ship as an energy source, but if a First Generation ship was used, it should be able to transport even further. With that much energy, the device will explode and the destination will be impossible to specify..." He thought it was an ingenious plan. Jurai would never find out where he was headed. Warp somewhere unspecified with Ryoko, defeat her, and he would remain missing. At the time, he thought it was a brilliant solution. He found a reason to escape from Jurai. The plan made him excited.

He decided to go to Earth, where his mother was born. On Tenju was a garden that recreated her homeland. She had told him stories of her home there since he was young. The thought that he could see that planet and even go there made his heart beat faster. So much so that his upcoming battle with Ryoko did not bother him…

"So I failed to seize the Tsunami Unit… I wonder what Kagato's face will be like." Just report the truth, Ryoko thought. It did not matter what he thought. He could come up with a plan himself. She was his tool. Tools did not have emotions.

Kagato only lectured the minimum amount necessary for Ryoko to carry out the mission as a sophisticated tool. But being in contact with society had brought her information. Ryoko may have been just a tool before, but a faint sense of self had arisen within her.

And at the same time, emotions.

At first, Ryoko did not feel any remorse about killing people. That did not mean she killed indiscriminately. She did not feel any pleasure in taking a life, and moreover, she was admonished by Kagato, who considered actions that were unrelated to carrying out objectives as inefficient. She eventually began to look forward to Kagato's orders. That was the dawning of her own emotions and ego. She desired to see emotional fluctuations in others. In that sense, this was the period during which she was most cold towards those who tried to thwart her. But even that was in the past. Anger, hatred, fear; the emotions directed at her had become too predictable.

I'm tired of it. They all make the same faces all the time... Kagato no longer made any comment on whatever she did, as long as she followed his orders. For him, even her emotions were objects of his research, she thought. The only thing she was forbidden to do was defy orders.

Even trying was pointless. I hate wasting time. She could see the puppet strings twining around her. In actuality, continuing to accept Kagato's orders was diminishing her budding feelings, cutting off her growth. But Ryoko desired emotion. The apathetic tried many things in search of thrills and pleasures. Drugs did not work. They were broken down the moment they were absorbed by her body, and she hated the rancid stench of those types of humans.

Her lack of a distinguished palate thwarted her gluttony. She simply needed to fill her stomach to satiety. She could get properly drunk on her favored spirits if she did not let her body break the alcohol down.

As for her sex drive—she tried various things, but being a famous pirate meant most prospective partners fled at the sight of her. Even if she hid her identity, most lost their nerve when they saw her eyes, and it had become tedious. Directly stimulating the brain through senses of sight, sound, and touch did not work, as there was some kind of security shield on her brain. Therefore, she did not get much satisfaction from sex or masturbation.

She found much more pleasure in destruction. By destroying things, she could witness the emotions of those who protected them, those who escaped, the fleeing bystanders—they were all so expressive. She never felt in danger herself. Killing was one directional, no different from play. She would rather have fun. She remembered Ayeka, her emotions raw and bare.

That girl made me laugh...

It had been a while since she felt her lips twist into a smile. Soon she was laughing out loud.

Ryoko clicked her tongue as she fired volleys to keep the Juraian fleet in check. They were all around her but staying neither too close nor too far. "They're plotting something. Ryo-Ohki, show me the star charts for a 100-light-year radius and his flight path so far."

"Meow." Ryo-Ohki displayed the star chart on the monitor instantaneously, and Ryoko noticed that Yosho was using the fleet to lead her to a specific location. There was even a giant transport system there.

"I get it." Ryoko let it happen because of her unprecedented experience decades ago, of fighting Kirito, the ship of the current Emperor of Jurai. She had enjoyed that battle. Funaho, the ship Yosho was chasing her with, had the same powers. If he desired a duel, that was favorable for her.

Ryoko reduced speed and waited. She opened a channel and

hailed Funaho. Yosho's face appeared on her screen at once. "Hey, where are you taking me, my Prince?"

"I wanted to show you my mother's homeland... Ha ha, I sound like I'm making a proposal."

"You're sure you can afford to be so relaxed? Fine, I accept." His eyes reminded her of her own... She did not know why she thought so, and it made her a little angry. She wanted to obliterate him, right now. Ryoko ordered Ryo-Ohki to fly into the waiting transporter. Funaho followed her, and there was a slight shock, like tripping on a pebble. Yosho did not notice it was Ryoko's pod.

The transporter exploded with the pressure of the two high-energy ships, and they disappeared light-years away. Hyperspace travel lasted only an instant. In less than a blink of an eye, Funaho exited into normal space. Yosho saw before him a planet with large rings, referred to the star charts, and confirmed that it was Earth's solar system.

"Where's Ryo-Ohki?" He searched for the other ship, lost in the time-space fluctuation.

"This bridge sure is different."

Yosho whirled around at the unexpected voice behind him, only to see Ryoko standing there. But then she vanished again. She stepped in with astounding agility and swung her sword of light energy. Yosho dodged by a hair; Funaho formed a distortion field around Ryoko and tossed her into the residential quarters. First Generation ships contained a subspace living area within. It was generally to protect against outside attacks, but this time it was the reverse. Yosho gripped his Master Key and transported there, and confronted Ryoko, waiting with her sword of light.

"Very clever."

"We can fight to our hearts' content here. Though I would've preferred to get a glimpse of Earth first!" A sword of light extended from Yosho's Master Key as well, as the two beams crossed in a shower of sparks. Ryoko was an order of magnitude more powerful in terms of raw strength, but her skills, accustomed to crushing foes by brute force alone, were artless at best. Yosho's techniques were honed over years, whereas Ryoko was self-taught. But even if Yosho evaded her attacks and leapt into striking range with only the power of the Master Key, Ryoko's defenses bounced him off. Yosho ended up being on the defensive.

Yosho used his own afterimages as bait to approach from her blind spot, but the damage was accumulating bit by bit from Ryoko, who lashed out in all directions. Ryoko's energy blasts, which were more powerful than that of a First Generation ship, though inefficient when fired in all directions, had the power to obliterate Yosho if he had been without Funaho's backup.

"Hah! You can't even scratch me with those attacks!!" She acted tough, but she was not able to anticipate most of Yosho's moves and was thus forced to attack in all directions.

"It seems that way." Three shining wings appeared in front of Yosho to reflect Ryoko's attacks.

"Light Hawk Wings?!" Since her previous battle with Emperor Azusa was ship-to-ship, she had not considered that Light Hawk Wings could be produced by an individual. If her multidirectional attacks were not going to work, being unable to follow his moves, Ryoko had no chance. "Crap!!" She tried to escape upwards in a panic, but as the thought was forming in her mind, Yosho was already behind her. He transformed the Light Hawk Wings into a blade of light and severed the jewel in Ryoko's right wrist. It was a feat only possible with backup from a Royal Tree and with Yosho's expert skill.

"One down!" With that, the jewel was sealed in the hilt of the Master Key. Ryoko screamed, lost her balance, and fell. With the removal of one jewel, the other two lost control. Since Yosho was using the Light Hawk Wings, the containment field of the living quarters was weakened and unable to withstand the violent torrent of power streaming from the jewels. Fissures formed in the subspace field. "Oh no, this won't last."

Yosho took another jewel from Ryoko—but this restored her power balance. Ryoko withdrew but fired an energy blast from the remaining jewel with everything she had. Yosho switched the sword back to a shield but was subjected to the extra energy that could not be deflected. He held on to the Master Key until Ryoko was transported, but he could not take it anymore and went down on his knees.

The scenery around him switched to Funaho's bridge. "I'm sorry, Funaho. I'm giving you back the Light Hawk Wings. Ryo-Ohki is coming...!!"

To prove his words, a beam flashed from Ryo-Ohki on the monitor. Because he had taken two jewels from Ryoko, Ryo-Ohki's defenses were clearly weakened, but her attack power had not diminished. The slight delay in reaction speed he saw when faced with Ryo-Ohki was now absent.

Funaho deployed the Light Hawk Wings and started to hammer away at Ryo-Ohki. "Good! This might work." Just then, a violent vibration shook Funaho's hull. It was a direct hit by Ryo-Ohki.

"A direct hit?! But the Light Hawk Wings are deployed!" Yosho hastily confirmed this on the monitors, seeing the three Light Hawk Wings. The next moment, there was another strike. "That's...impossible!!"

Ryo-Ohki's attacks were passing through the Light Hawk Wings. It was the same phenomenon as the time Azusa, Yosho's father battled Kirito and Ryo-Ohki. The damage to both ships, battling without defenses, began to affect navigation.

How long had they been fighting? Yosho was wrestling with severe pain when he saw the planet appear from behind the moon. "That...must be Earth!" The planet where his mother was born. The planet of blue waters. Yosho stared at its beauty for a short time but came back to his senses at Funaho's pleas. Ryo-Ohki suddenly filled the entire field of view on the screen. *A suicide attack!* As the thought ran through his mind, a tremendous shock shook Funaho's bridge.

Ryo-Ohki was wounded badly, and perhaps because she was a living spaceship, instinctively sought water, descending toward Earth without any input from Yosho. Yosho threw Funaho's weight against Ryo-Ohki to steer them towards a small island country. Funaho's outer hull was already destroyed, with no trace of its original structure left.

"Mrrgrowwl!" With her crystal glowing bright red and a horrific yowl, Ryo-Ohki flew across the night sky, crash-landing on the surface. Funaho's unit was also badly damaged, forcing a crash landing.

This is it... There was no guarantee the damaged core unit would withstand such a landing. *But if I may die on my mother's home world...*

He closed his eyes and vanished. Funaho had used the last of her strength to transport herself and Yosho.

"Yosho...kun... Yosho-kun..." He heard a voice from somewhere. She sat next to him, cupping her cheek in one hand while she poked him in the cheek with a finger. A girl with strong force of will in her eyes. She eased the suffering inside him. "Yosho-kun..." Misty-eyed, she rubbed her cheek against his, just like a cat expressing her deepest affections... He did not want to part from her. He wanted to stay by her side, feeling her warmth. But it was not to be. Her tears were testament. "I love you... Yosho..."

"Airi-dono!" Yosho grabbed the hand in front of him and realized that it did not belong to the woman calling to him from the depths of his consciousness but a girl he had never seen before. "No, it's not her..."

"Oh..." The girl turned bright red and withdrew her hand and hurriedly left the room. Yosho's mind was still in a haze, and he watched her silently. Once his head started to clear, he pushed himself up to better assess the situation. He was resting in a room.

The house was old but tasteful and comfortable, and reflective of its caretaker's character. From between the sliding shoji doors the girl had left open, he saw gorgeous fall foliage.

"It's so beautiful…" Yosho felt like he knew this place. As he gazed outside, a bright red leaf from a garden maple fluttered down by his pillow, tossed by the breeze. He picked it up and studied it.

"I'm glad you're awake."

Yosho looked up to see an old man sliding the door shut behind him. He was probably the master of this house. "I am deeply grateful for your care while I was unconscious," he bowed.

The old man shook his head. "The one who found you was my granddaughter, Kasumi." Yosho looked over towards the young girl he saw earlier.

"Um… I-I'll go get some water." When their eyes met, she blushed and ran off. She stepped outside and tripped over nothing. She popped back up, dusted herself off, and looked over at Yosho, her face still beet red. She hastily got up and started running again.

Yosho could not help laughing, as she reminded him of a puppy.

"She can be rather clumsy. Please don't mind her."

"Oh no, she deserves thanks for saving my life. My name is Masaki Yosho."

The old man burst out laughing upon hearing his name for some reason. He apologized, saying his name was Tairoh. "I'm sorry. This must be some kind of fate…"

"Fate, you say?"

"See that mountain? It has the same name as you." He pointed towards a nearby peak.

Yosho raised himself up and looked around. The scenery was the same as his mother's garden. "Where am I...?"

"I apologize if I'm mistaken, but are you Funaho's... No, that's not possible. Forget I ever mentioned it."

At Tairoh's words, Yosho realized where he was, as well as who this old man and the young girl were. "Tairoh-dono, I..." Just as he started to tell him the truth, they heard Kasumi's scream from afar.

Tairoh scratched his head and said, "She probably tripped again somewhere..."

"Oh no!" Yosho stood up with a shout. He had not confirmed whether Ryoko was alive or dead. He overcame the pain of his wounds and ran towards the voice with Tairoh.

"Wh-what is that?! A woman...or an ogre?" They were close to the crater where Ryo-Ohki had crashed. There, Ryoko, covered in wounds, was holding Kasumi. With an exultant smile, she held out her hand.

"Give me back...my jewels..."

"Ryoko, let her go. If you want them, take them from me by force. You're a pirate."

"Give them back... I can't control my hands, heh heh."

"I-I can't breathe."

"Stop it!"

Paying no heed to Yosho, Ryoko tightened her grip on Kasumi's neck. She really did not have control over her hand.

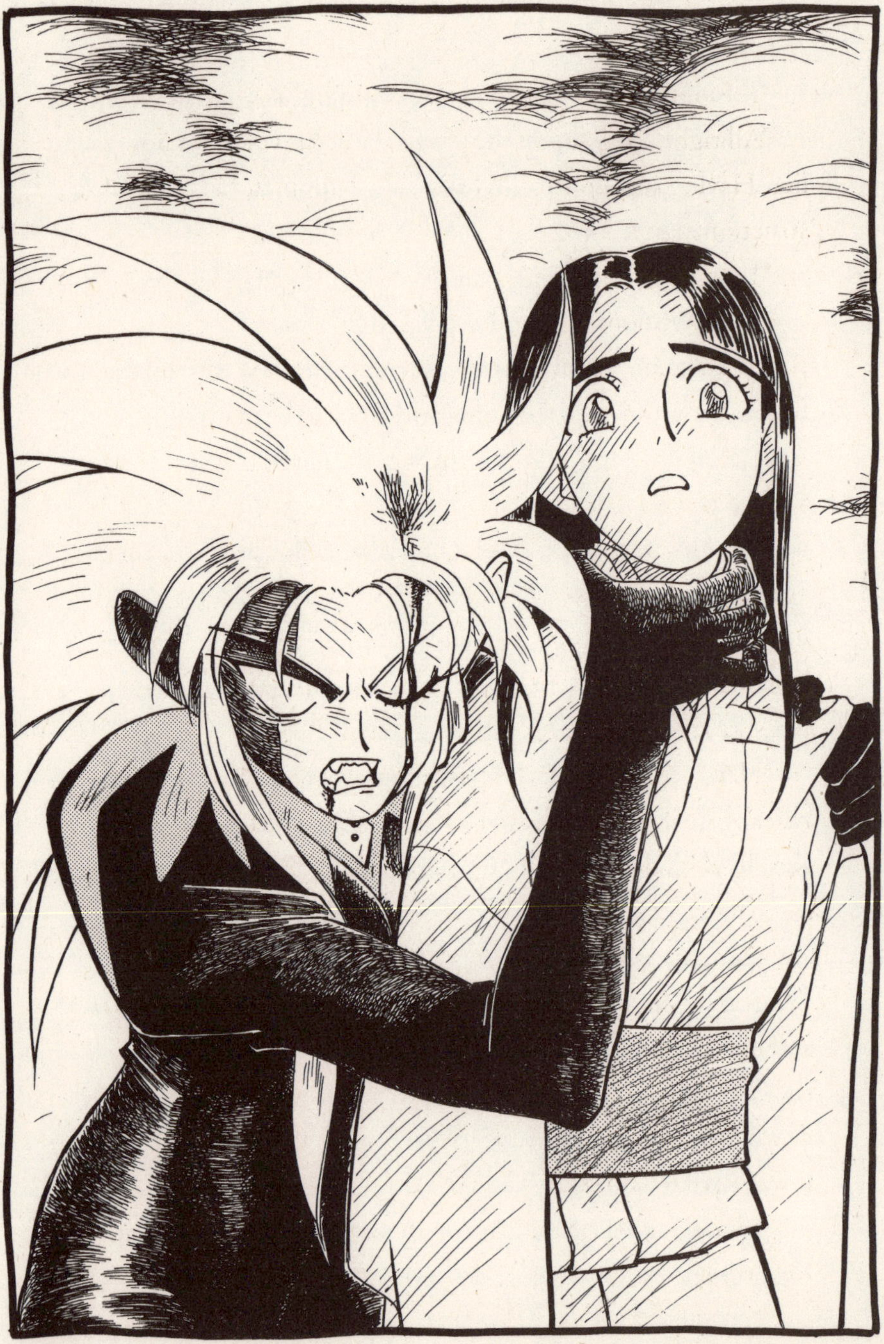

"Kasumi!" Tairoh shouted heartrendingly.

"All right, I'll give you the jewels!" But his voice did not reach her. Having lost control, Ryoko acted upon the instinct of destruction alone.

"I can't bre-"

"Stop it, nooo!!"

At that moment, it happened. As if it was foreordained... Kasumi's bosom radiated light and knocked Ryoko away.

"...!!"

Yosho used that moment to take out his Master Key, enduring the pain and thrust his sword into Ryoko's neck. Ryoko struggled and gurgled, and stretched her hand out toward Yosho, baring her sharp claws. There was a crazed smile on her face. She was in pain, but this was the first time she'd had this much fun. It was a pleasure she had never experienced before.

"Heh, heh heh, ha ha ha... Kya ha ha ha ha!!" She laughed maniacally. Yosho sealed the last jewel from her neck into his Master Key. Ryoko's flailing limbs grew quieter, then stopped moving.

There was a sigh of relief—and then, Ryoko opened her eyes wide and assaulted Yosho. The two of them vanished. Or so it seemed to Tairoh and Kasumi's eyes. But around them were sounds of explosions and roaring wind, and in less than a minute, they appeared before them again. Ryoko stood, while Yosho was down on one knee. It seemed like the victor was obvious. But then it was Ryoko who collapsed like a puppet with severed strings.

"What's going on...?!" Yosho, panting, looked at his Master Key, which was glowing in reaction to something. Kasumi, also having sensed something, took out a comb from her bosom. Seeing it, Yosho opened his eyes wide. "That's from a Royal Tree..."

The comb, a memento of her late mother, was the one Funaho had left her younger sister. "Fate..." Yosho mumbled, holding the Master Key. A return to one's origins. Those born into the Masaki House shared a destiny. They would always wander and face change.

Azusa

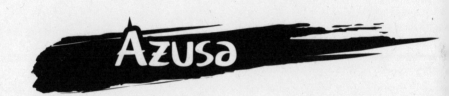

B Y THE TIME any trace of Yosho, who had left in pursuit of Ryoko, was gone, the Imperial Family connected to a conference call through the network of Royal Trees. The topic was the report submitted by Tatsua, the commander at the time of the attack.

"What a disgrace! The main forces may have been absent, but allowing a single pirate vessel into the home world, even damaging Tenju! Yosho-dono let her escape, and now both are missing. This is unprecedented in the entire history of Jurai. How will you take responsibility?!" Shuzan spat, his words fast and furious. He had conveniently arrived two hours after Ryoko left Jurai. He actually seemed to be smiling. Shuzan was unable to accept the facts put forward in Tatsua's report. To accept them would mean Ryoko and Ryo-Ohki were not *mere* pirates. What he needed to do was to transform this meeting into a forum for pinning liability on House Masaki for this deplorable affair.

"They were no mere pirates," said Tatsua, infuriated by

Shuzan's outburst. "That wasn't a case of illegal modifications on refurbished military vessels. And they knew what they were doing, coming after the Royal Trees. They were clearly backed by a large organization, be it the pirates' guild or another nation!"

"Hmph! I'm saying there are problems in the data in this report. It was Ayeka-dono's ship going out of control that allowed entry into Tenju to begin with!"

"It's indisputable that they had the power to make a raid on the home world!"

"The existence of such power is unthinkable! Who could develop such a thing? The most likely is the Galaxy Academy... But they would never attack Jurai. If they could, those philosophers would've smugly published it already!"

While Tatsua and Shuzan's exchange of opinions (which is to say, quarrel) continued, Emperor Azusa and Utsutsumi, the head of House Kamiki, silently observed the state of things. Utsutsumi, with his instincts as a self-made soldier, knew that this report was correct. He wanted to stop Shuzan's absurd accusations, but his particular feelings towards Azusa and Funaho stayed his hand. *This is a job for the Emperor of Jurai. If he cannot even get this under control, it's better for Jurai if he'd just hand the title over to someone else.*

Sensing Utsutsumi's feelings, Azusa interrupted Shuzan and Tatsua. "Enough!"

"But!" Shuzan objected.

"That ship—Ryo-Ohki—is no ordinary ship." He told them how he once fought Ryo-Ohki, back in the day. Even so, Shuzan and his henchmen continued to dispute Ryoko's powers.

It was Misaki who eventually lost her patience. *This man is a blockhead for not knowing the true powers of a First Generation Tree.* She started to yell, "You are..."

Seto's carefully controlled voice broke in and quelled Misaki's rant. "How unfortunate. If only Shuzan-dono had been on Jurai at the time, he wouldn't have allowed this *mere pirate* to create such havoc. Isn't that right? He said his comm was jammed. Even though he was closer than Yosho-dono. It's too bad!" Each word dripped with sarcasm. She would generally never neglect Utsutsumi, but she was also fed up with this.

Shuzan realized that the tide was about to turn against him and hastily winked at one of his henchmen, who equally hastily changed the subject, "We can argue about responsibility at the inquiry. For now, correctly assessing the situation should come first..."

In exchange for disregarding the suspicion that he purposefully delayed his arrival on Jurai, they dismissed House Masaki's responsibility for the failures in defense. After the transmission was over, Shuzan vented his anger on his own bridge, but once "demon princess" Seto stated her case, pursuing it further would only backfire. He had no choice but to give up.

The final decision left Jurai's current defenses to Shuzan, and the others continued their voyages. This was so that other countries would not be alerted to the attack because of their rushing home. They also had the opportunity to gather information abroad. This event was reported internationally as a training exercise for defense of the home world. The damage was too great for anyone to believe it was just a training exercise, but at word that Seto had been the sponsor, everyone understood.

The official meeting now over, on board the Jurai Emperor's ship were Azusa, Funaho, Misaki, and through the First Generation Tree special channel, a visual of Seto. With these four, the *true* Jurai Supreme Council could begin.

"You dummy!" That was Seto, referring to her daughter's careless actions in the council.

"I'm sorry, Mother. I'm sorry, Oneesama," Misaki said in a pitiful voice, her head hung low. Laying it out to Shuzan meant he would not do anything to Misaki, out of fear towards Seto, but he would turn his resultant discontent towards Funaho. That was what she was mad about.

"It's all right, Misaki-chan. It made me happy."

"I'm sorry," Azusa apologized, and Funaho smiled her understanding. With the Emperor of Jurai and the power of a First Generation ship, it would be easy to remove Shuzan. But the Emperor was not a dictator and existed to protect his family. And no matter how problematic he was, Shuzan was still family.

"Shuzan and my husband sure take peace for granted, not appreciating the Emperor with his First Generation Tree," Seto sighed.

"Let us get to the point, Seto-dono."

"All right." Seto relayed her data to each monitor. "Tatsua-dono rightly had calm, objective judgment. My analysis of the situation reached the same conclusions."

"So Ryoko and Ryo-Ohki had powers superior to even a First Generation ship... Seto-dono, do you think they're related to Tsunami in some way?"

"Aw, that was supposed to be the highlight of my report!" Seto pouted as Azusa hit the nail on the head. Like mother, like daughter.

With a sigh, Azusa continued, "I was concerned by the fact that all the Third Generation ships on Jurai hesitated to attack, and the Fourth Generation ships that basically have no will were also slightly slower to react. When I battled Ryo-Ohki, I too felt a slight delay in reaction speed. I was injured at the time, and I had assumed it was due to the slower transmission, so I hadn't included it in my report to Seto-dono. If even First Generation ships hesitate to attack, there's nobody else but Tsunami... Well, I'm sure Seto-dono has more surprises up her sleeve. Otherwise she wouldn't put in a call for a meeting of the Supreme Council."

"Azusa-chan, you're getting more boring," grumbled Seto morosely. "Actually...I've been studying Ryoko and Ryo-Ohki ever since I received Azusa-dono's report. Ryoko wasn't as famous on Jurai, where we're protected by our powerful ships powered by the Royal Trees, but she posed quite a threat in other star systems."

"I'm not surprised, with that power."

"And another thing. She specialized in robbing artifacts from ancient ruins and seizing information from ruins of pre-historical civilizations. There is little of that within Jurai territories, another reason why Ryoko wasn't very well known. To get straight to the point, she wasn't sent by some country or organization."

"Then Kagato is also unaffiliated."

"Are you saying an individual built that?"

"There's more. The profile of Kagato only went back 5,000 years. Nothing is known about him before he showed up on the most wanted list. But that was the biggest problem."

"What had he done?"

"He annihilated an entire brigade of some idiots from a certain major country who were poaching on a planet designated as a special protection reserve. By himself." Azusa was at a loss for words, as this was a fairly famous incident in inner circles. "The important thing is, there was someone else on that planet there for conservation research. Who do you think it was?" Seto asked happily.

"Mother." Misaki immediately pointed to Seto. It was a joke, implying Seto could be involved in such an extreme incident.

"That person..." Seto, Funaho, and Azusa huddled to talk. Beside them was Misaki, crying with a lump on her head from Seto. "...was Hakubi Washu."

Funaho's eyes were round in astonishment. "Washu?! You mean the founder of the Galaxy Academy? That... eccentric?"

"You mean back when it was Jurai's Imperial Academy," said Azusa.

"Yes. And the assistant with Washu on the planet at the research institute was called Kagato." Seto showed them a photograph of Washu and her assistant, except it was a woman.

Azusa rubbed his jaw and frowned. "That looks different from the one I met... But it must be one and the same person."

"I've gathered evidence on who Kagato the assistant was. She was unaffiliated with any organization."

"But... I've seen this face before, Mother..." Misaki stared at Kagato's face, puzzled.

"Isn't this the one?" Seto brought out another photograph, also taken with Washu.

"What's this...?" Misaki looked at Seto quizzically.

"Washu's expression..." Funaho murmured. Like she said, Washu's expression was completely different. One was tense, and the other was peaceful and relaxed. "These two are different people?"

"Yes. The second picture is of Akara Naja, Washu's friend. Kagato seems to be her clone."

"What happened to the original?"

"About 5000 years ago, she died in a pirate attack during an archaeological excavation on uninhabited planet K1190... Well, technically missing, since her body was never found. Circumstantial evidence states she shouldn't be alive. She was supposed to have been a philosopher rivaling Washu."

"K1190? Isn't that Mother's..."

Seto nodded, "Yes... where my foster father rescued me when I was six years old."

"You, Seto-dono?!"

"There were a number of treasure hunters besides Akara Naja's excavation team. My foster father, Kamiki Ushio, annihilated the pirates and rescued the survivors. I was an orphan of those treasure hunters, though I had lost my memories through the shock of the attack." Seto smiled sadly, then smoothly switched back to her usual smile. "Anyway, the problem is with Washu. She was left in front of an orphanage on Kanamitsu, a planet in Juraian territory, 20,000 years ago. The rest is a cliché. She was estimated to be around three when she was taken in, but she didn't have any memories. Nothing was ever found out about her past. She tried a lot of things in her Galaxy Academy days to make herself remember, but nothing worked. The only concern is this." The screen showed the three red jewels.

Azusa, suspicious, wondered, "What's this?"

"The only things she had with her. I can understand how nobody thought the possessions of a child were important. But it was a little careless." Seto pressed some buttons and brought an image of Ryoko up on a screen. "When I examined the databanks of the Galaxy Police and the battle data on Jurai, I found that Ryoko and Ryo-Ohki's energy source is located in her wrists and neck. Look." The three locations were magnified.

"What's this?!" Everyone but Seto opened their eyes wide. What was shown were the same red jewels as Washu had.

"I don't know if they're the exact ones that Washu had, but even if they were appropriated or replicated, it's unmistakable they're the same thing... It's a shame it was 20,000 years ago. Might as well go ask Tsunami."

"Her past holds the answer," said Funaho.

"In the 15,000 years after, I haven't been able to find anything that's considered related, for now... But I'm amazed a single person has done so much. I'd say she's the most powerful person I've ever seen or heard of. I sense consistency or a policy in her principles; at least, that's my impression. There's no sign that there's been any outside influence on her ideology."

The trouble was, Azusa thought, that Seto's impression was most credible.

"In conclusion, this assistant is using something Washu-dono herself had developed for personal purposes. What we feared the most hasn't become reality. Other countries haven't placed as high an importance on it."

"If they find out about what happened in Jurai, things will change."

"The simulations show that Jurai is the most likely to capture Ryo-Ohki. Specifically, the Royal Trees. Other countries would have to pull off something on a large scale. And that increases the chances of leaking information... It makes sabotage too easy."

"Mother... you look like you're enjoying yourself."

"I would think most countries would rather destroy them than give them up to someone else... In any case, we can't do anything until we figure out where Ryoko and Kagato are."

Azusa nodded, "So with Ryoko, we're going to avoid the worst case scenario of upsetting the balance of military force. Now the question is how to obtain this technology before other countries... Please continue with the investigation, Seto-dono, Misaki."

"This profile on Washu-dono was written up like a biography by a playful employee of mine. It's quite an interesting read. Check it out."

This was how the first Supreme Council on Ryoko ended. They were not able to find the whereabouts of Yosho or Ryoko. They sent a secret investigative team to Earth, but they could not outsmart a First Generation Tree's cover-up and had to return without finding any clues.

It had been six years since Yosho went missing. Since there was no information on Ryoko popping up, the leading theory among the Imperial Family was that they had perished at each other's hands. It was then that it happened.

"Again?" said Seto, who had come to visit the executive office at House Kamiki.

"Now don't say that, he's worried about Ayeka in his way." Before Utsutsumi were holographs of several young men. Shuzan had recently started to bring in prospective marriage partners, after the Emperor of Jurai officially declared the engagement between Yosho and Ayeka be annulled. Ayeka rejected every one of them, but after a conference with the heads of Houses, they selected some candidates for matchmaking interviews, the first steps to an arranged marriage. And once it was arranged, it could not be refused.

Even after six years of her brother missing, Ayeka's feelings had not changed from the moment she last saw him. Rather, because she could not see him, her ideals grew all the more lofty, an unstoppable force inside her. Perhaps it was true that this was not genuine love but feelings that she had built up for more than a decade and could not forget so easily.

The day before the marriage candidate selected for Ayeka by Houses Kamiki and Masaki was announced, Ayeka decided to leave Jurai and go on a journey to find Yosho. She was a woman of Jurai's Masaki House, who thought nothing of abandoning her home.

The hull destroyed in the battle with Ryoko was repaired, and when she exited Jurai "for final adjustments," she was going to switch the bio-signature emitted from the ship (with which her position would be ascertained) with a dummy ship onto which a cutting from Ryu-oh was placed, to trick the surveilling eyes back on Jurai. The key she fashioned from Ryu-oh's amber in the shape of a headband fit nicely on her forehead. The perfect plan (in Ayeka's thinking) to run away from Jurai was complete.

The problem was Yosho's location. Ayeka knew he could not be found by searching blindly, and she herself would quickly be found by Jurai and sent back home. These things were better left to the experts. Luckily, the search for Yosho had continued. The information was controlled by the secret network of Royal Trees, and since Ayeka's Ryu-oh was a Second Generation Tree, it could receive information without directly accessing Tenju and could therefore do so without being detected.

"It's perfect! ♥" she beamed. The thought patterns of a girl in love were simplistic.

On the day of the plan's execution, Ayeka secretly departed Jurai, left her Guardians, Azaka and Kamidake, in control, and entered the hibernation chamber. She had no idea it would last seven hundred years.

An amateur could never evade Jurai's surveillance network. However, Ayeka also did not know that they were able to successfully give them the slip through the power of Sasami (and thus Tsunami), who had stowed away out of concern for her sister.

Meanwhile, on Jurai, things were naturally in an uproar. Not only Ayeka but Sasami had gone missing without a note. A search team was formed immediately, but it was impossible to locate Ryu-oh, once under Tsunami's protection. The situation on Jurai was grave in a different sense. There was no way the methods Ayeka used could have deceived Jurai's security. All the organizations from ground control to the intelligence department underwent a thorough review, in case the stunt had been performed under someone's guidance, but nobody suspicious could be found.

The one with the most mixed emotions was none other than Seto herself. "Why, why, whyyyy?? I'm so tired…" Her secret detection mechanism, touted as the most powerful on Jurai, had been bested. No mastermind, not even a spy, could be found. There was no way this could have been done without so much as a trace. Scrutiny of the Imperial Family was supposed to be extraordinary.

"Could it be…Tsunami?" There was no other answer. "Were you worried about Ayeka-chan?" Those simple words were the answer to everything. Seto felt intuitively that Ayeka and Sasami were safe. But ever since the first leader of Jurai met Tsunami, there had never been a case of Tsunami herself taking action.

"What's about to happen?" Seto felt a great fluctuation of fate. "Uh-oh…I had forgotten about *her*." Considering the coming kerfuffle, she felt a headache coming on. "Funaho-dono… I hope she doesn't keep things bottled up."

There was one other person who most decidedly did not have peace of mind: Ayeka and Sasami's grandfather, Utsutsumi. With his two most beloved granddaughters gone, he was in a panic. And it mattered that the whole thing was Azusa's son, Yosho's fault.

"That was when everything went wrong." Simple but fearless, and highly trusted by others, Utsutsumi had a thing against Funaho (more accurately, Azusa). "This wouldn't have been a problem if she had been Second Empress," he muttered. He knew that it was selfish. But after Ayeka was born, and seeing his granddaughter so happily engaged to Yosho, his ill feelings had gradually faded away. Then Sasami was born. If this contentment had continued, Utsutsumi would have had nothing left to be desired.

Even he knew he was being stupid. What might have been the smallest thing, seen from someone else's perspective, had ruined everything for him and even affected the future of an entire country.

"This isn't good!" He sighed deeply and left the executive office to head to the meeting.

As everyone present in the meeting expected, there was great upset about Ayeka and Sasami's disappearance. And it was a matter of course that all topics of discussion turned into criticism of Funaho. There was no help from Azusa, who had to remain neutral as Emperor. Funaho endured taking heavier criticism from Shuzan than ever before.

Then Shuzan made the crucial assertion: "The same as the First Prince... He had a First Generation ship, and yet he let that pirate escape. Now he's missing. The apple doesn't fall far from the tree."

Funaho could put up with criticism of herself, but when it came to her son, she could not keep quiet. She walked over to

Shuzan and dumped a cup of sake over him. This was a challenge to a duel. Until now, he could not bring himself to challenge a woman, much less someone from another world who had not received much combat training, as a victory would only reflect poorly on him. Being offered one on a silver platter was a different story. Shuzan was ecstatic.

"Are you sure? You can put up a proxy." He left her an escape route, since he knew she could do no such thing.

"And this is no verbal quarrel," Funaho said. Shuzan shivered with indignation at this additional provocation.

Misaki watched this confrontation apprehensively and noticed her mother Seto had a big twitching smile on her face. "You plotted this, Mother."

"I don't know what you're talking about. Ho ho ho."

Right as this touchy situation peaked, in came Utsutsumi, entering late, right in front of Funaho and Shuzan. He glared at the two of them and sighed. "We're all idiots. Me *and* Shuzan-dono. Funaho-dono was caught up in this mess for ridiculous reasons; she can't do this sober." He ordered the attendants to bring several large casks. It was his treasured stash of the finest sake. "Let us not stand on ceremony."

This was turning into a bar fight. Juraians used to be pirates, so this was nothing out of the ordinary, and the customs remained to this day. If something could not be decided by a discussion, things came to a head by force. Reason was cast aside to let them vent with everything they had.

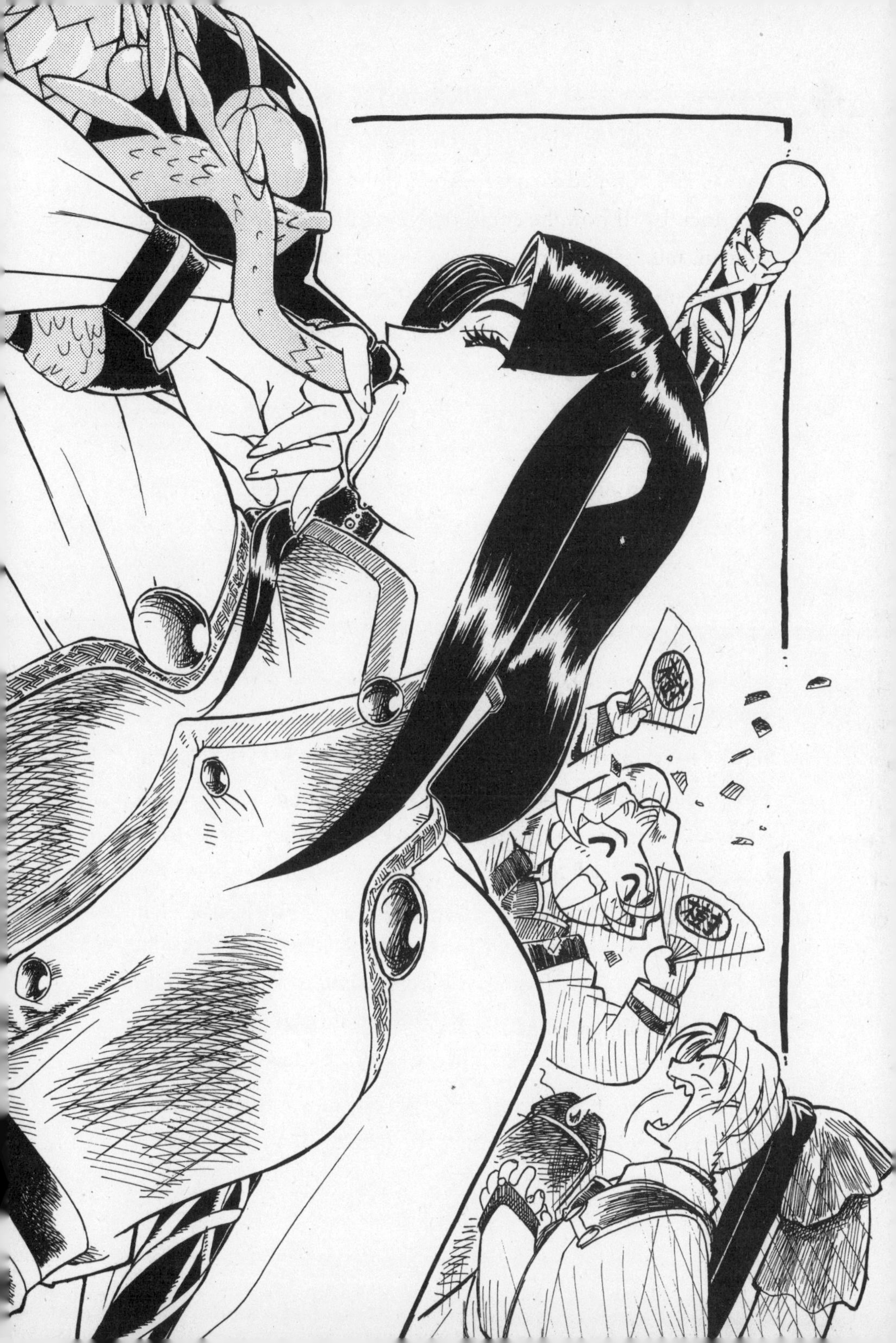

Funaho was given a large club to face Shuzan with, and she abruptly upended a large bottle. Seeing this, Shuzan grinned. "Are you preparing an excuse for when you lose?"

"Come on, you mother#!*@er!" She might have been drunk already. Azusa and Misaki averted their eyes at Funaho's uncharacteristic behavior. They knew her predispositions.

Infuriated, Shuzan charged. But in the blink of an eye he was walloped, dunked into a casket, and knocked unconscious. It was not that Shuzan was weak. Funaho was extraordinarily powerful. Watching this, Seto screeched with joy.

"Well, this is a surprise. Did she take lessons from Misaki? But this isn't enough to best me," Utsutsumi downed a small cask to liven things up and charged at Funaho. But just like Shuzan, Utsutsumi was easily subdued and tossed down in front of Misaki, who was dutifully sitting politely. "Wh-what?!"

"Father, you had the wrong idea. I didn't teach her. She spars with me," Misaki chuckled.

"What?!"

"With a staff, she's more powerful than Misaki-chan," Seto said nonchalantly. It meant Funaho was more powerful than Utsutsumi.

"What? Arg...!" Utsutsumi picked himself back up and rushed at Funaho, who was cackling with flushed cheeks. Nobody could stop her now, and that was the way this was supposed to be. Azusa decided to sit back and watch over his wife, his face twitching.

Funaho started to slow down, having drunk too much. "Uh-oh," said Azusa.

Misaki said to Utsutsumi, "Father, you should wind down..."

Utsutsumi thought he now had the upper hand and raised his club towards Funaho, but he was blown away again. Shuzan, now awake, followed into the fray, uttering a strange squeal.

"Mother..."

"It's fine. It's a casual affair anyway," answered Seto, leaving Shuzan and his followers, sealing the transport pod to the great hall. "This is a good lesson for the others to learn."

"Mother...you scare me." Misaki shuddered at Seto's tittering. From the sealed hall, an angry roar, sounds of destruction, and general pandemonium could be heard.

"It's started. Come on, hurry!!" Seto spread out the volumes of sake and food she brought from the hall and camped on the nearby deck with the best view of the hall. She started the Great Pandemonium Spectacle party, hosted by her, and began pulling in the passing ladies-in-waiting and security guards.

When Funaho got drunk, she showed strength not even Azusa and Misaki together could handle. The recoil from her days of suppression was frightful.

Members of the Jurai Imperial Family could receive backup from royal ships during combat. And Funaho could forcibly extract backup not only from her own ship but Misaki's. Not even Misaki herself could receive backup from Funaho's ship. Once she was drunk and reason flew out the window, the ships' powers streamed into her automatically. She was basically a berserker. Even with an anti-energy force field, nothing could block two Second Generation ships. An hour later, the matter came to a close with the complete destruction of the great hall.

"It's still too dangerous to approach…" Seto's party continued for several more hours until the alcohol was out of Funaho's system.

In the hospital room, Seto sat beside the mummified Utsutsumi, who had bandages around his entire body. "Have you learned your lesson now?"

"Hmph. I see you made sure to escape by yourself."

"You reap what you sow. Why don't you just admit already that you have a problem?"

"What do you mean?"

"You probably consider yourself a disgrace."

"Yes… Yes, I do!" Utsutsumi closed his eyes and declared. "But I asked Misaki that day if she wanted to be the First Empress. She smiled happily and said 'yes.' I wanted to do things the way she wanted! And now look, Misaki is all doting on Funaho-dono. 'Oh, I'm going to be Second Empress after Oneesama.'" He clenched his fist, his mouth turned down at the corners. Misaki made this same gesture often.

"*Well*. I knew you were an idiot but not this much. Right, Misaki, Funaho-dono? Don't you agree?" Seto called towards the door, and there stood Misaki and Funaho with bouquets of flowers.

"Gack!!" Seto stopped Utsutsumi from hiding under the blanket. "Seto, I can't believe you!!" he shouted pathetically, turning bright red.

"Dear."

"Shut up! Shut up!"

"Father...I'm sorry. Thank you." Misaki hugged him.

"I'm sorry I didn't realize, I..." Funaho cast her eyes downwards apologetically.

"I have nothing to say, I lost the duel. Don't mind me." Having only himself to blame for his humiliation, he no longer had the willpower to remain defiant. And now with a beautiful woman making such a face at him... He had long felt a strong inferiority complex toward Funaho. All his anger transferred to Azusa, that idiot, as this was how he could deceive himself. "Besides, nobody will defy you again. Including me. Ha ha ha!!"

"I'm glad you were able to sweep this under the rug," whispered Seto in his ear so nobody else heard. Utsutsumi could only laugh.

On Jurai, where pirate traditions remained strong, those who excelled in one thing were respected. That duel enabled Funaho to be accepted as a member of the Imperial Family. And that in turn cemented Azusa's status as Emperor of Jurai. Thanks to Seto, everything worked out.

Needless to say, nobody offered Funaho alcohol ever again.

Epilogue

Yosho was recuperating at Tairoh's. On Earth, several months had passed since the battle with Ryoko, and Funaho, the Royal Tree, had taken root at the base of the mountain. A Royal Tree that takes root loses its power. She would never fly again.

Yosho decided to live his life here with Kasumi. With Funaho's remaining energy, he retrieved the things he needed from his room in hyperspace. Once Funaho lost power, he would have no way to access it. He could have returned to Jurai immediately if he only sent a distress signal, but he had chosen to live his life on this planet.

Ryoko's jewels were taken from her, but she was not dead. Yosho created a force field in a rocky area close by and sealed her in. He did not know why he did not kill her. But he did see unexpected purity and beauty in her eyes. They reminded him of Ayeka... Yes, they were very childlike. Thinking of those eyes, he could not bring himself to hate her.

The damage incurred in the battle had caused rumors, creating a larger problem. Yosho was at a loss. Despite his unease, Tairoh and Kasumi were calm.

"You don't need to do anything."

"But there must've been witnesses. How should we explain…?"

"Leave it to us."

These lands were rife with legends of ogres to begin with. The terrified residents nearby who had witnessed Ryo-Ohki's red crystals and roaring that night easily believed that it had been a battle between an ogre and a warrior. It was the most sensible explanation to them. Things quieted down when a shrine was built to appease the ogre. Its establishment brought peace of mind to the people, and conveniently for Yosho, fear of the ogre kept people away.

A few years later, Yosho married Kasumi. It didn't abate his feelings for Airi, but she built a position in his heart similar to Airi's. They had three children and lived in tranquility for a while…but a curious phenomenon was a source of concern to Yosho. Royal Trees gradually weakened and lost their power when rooted in the ground. But Funaho did not lose any of her power even after decades. He soon guessed that it had to do with Ryoko's jewels. If they had been the source of Ryoko's energy, then it was very possible it was flowing into Funaho through the Master Key.

Royal Trees absorb energy from innumerable different dimensions through their roots. Or, more accurately, the roots converted this energy into a form unique to Royal Trees. This was only possible within its specialized containment unit, and this was why they lost power when rooted. But there was another way to maintain power: to receive a charge from another Royal Tree. But since it could not absorb it from the roots, they could only accept energy of the same kind.

"If the jewels are the source of energy... I can't think of anything else. Then the jewels must contain the same kind of energy as the Royal Trees." And Funaho was a First Generation Tree. To maintain her power, the power hidden in Ryoko's jewels would have to at least equal that of a First Generation Tree. It was hard to believe, but since she attacked the Jurai home world and fought on even terms with Funaho, there could be no doubt.

"I'm lucky that Funaho's not losing power. Thinking beyond that is pointless." Yosho thought this way because there was a more pressing problem: that of his children, who inherited his blood and thus would live far longer than other people on Earth. The other issue was that lifespan extension was possible because Funaho had not lost her power.

Kasumi lived many years but could not endure the concept of living in a different timeline than others. She rejected any further extensions at eighty years old and chose to die of old age. She was long-suffering and did not express her anxieties outwardly but would often seem pained. However, once she started to show signs of age, she became more emotionally stable and her expressions grew more peaceful, to Yosho's relief.

She died at the ripe old age of 138. For Kasumi, it was a long and happy enough life.

Based on conversations he had with her while she was alive,

Yosho decided something important. Kasumi especially desired that none besides Yosho should have their lifespans extended. Extending life with a First Generation Royal Tree enabled maintenance of youth, and even humans of Earth could live longer than a thousand years. But that was different from bio-fortification, and psychologically and physically they would remain human. Even if they were able to mentally endure the reality of living so many years, no amount of bio-fortification would prevent the destabilization of the body, and Kasumi knew this. As long as they lived on Earth, they would live long enough lives without doing a thing. It was dangerous to attempt to extend their lives further.

But Yosho was a bio-fortified Juraian, with a duty to monitor that Ryoko was kept safely sealed away. As a result, it did not take long to reach the conclusion that they should pretend that Funaho had lost power.

In any case, a long life on Earth caused a multitude of problems. The more descendants Yosho had, the harder it would be to remain detached from the outside world and the more rumors about his long life would spread. Fortunately, rumors were just that, and few fully trusted such tales. Especially while the transmission of information was undeveloped, details were easily lost or changed with precise interference. Once that village of longevity was closed off behind Funaho's force field, or erased from official maps, its credibility would vanish, and the rumors along with it. Curiosities were relegated to and buried in corners of memory unless they were physically proximate and involved in daily life.

EPILOGUE

Without specific memories, very few outside of the modern age had the capacity to verify such things.

But then there were people who had the wherewithal and tenacity of purpose to verify those rumors: the authority figures of the day. They made contact with Yosho in various ways to obtain the secrets of long life, but to protect himself and his clan, Yosho would have no mercy. Bio-fortified, and with the power of a First Generation Tree at full power, there was nowhere safe on Earth for those authority figures. Imbued with incredible fearsomeness, Yosho became a legend, and those in power along with any who aspired to great power gained a tacit understanding to regard Yosho as forbidden. Though even Yosho had to laugh when the fear turned into worship, and Yosho was deified and revered as a warrior god.

Those originally of different colors could not be dyed one color. There would always be distortions. To continue to live in a hidden village and cut off contact with the outside world was dangerous for Yosho's descendants. A while after Kasumi passed, Yosho decided to use Funaho's power to contact Kanemitsu at the Galaxy Academy. He was aware that he would be picked up by Seto's information network. The Emperor of Jurai's network had still not caught up to Seto's. That was a glimpse of Seto's ability, as desired as Jurai's Empress.

"It's been a while, Kanemitsu-dono."

"Are you Yosho…?!" The moment he uttered Yosho's name, Kanemitsu was abruptly kicked out of view.

"Yosho...kun. Are you really Yosho-kun? There's no doubt about it. Yosho-kun!!" The one who appeared instead...

"Airi...dono..." Yosho was at a loss for words. Airi, whom he had thought he would never see again, had appeared before him, beautifully matured into a woman. And Airi was enraptured by Yosho, all grown up into a strapping man, and she blushed. However...

"Why... you... idiot!!" Her angry bellow reverberated through the screen and through the mountains, sure to give birth to another legend about ogres. Yosho, who saw it coming, covered his ears. "You just covered your ears?! After all the worry you caused me..." Airi growled, about to explode.

"Airi-dono... calm down."

"Why you..." The moment she tried to yell again, a swarm of Funaho puppies flew out from her ring. "Squee! Funaho-chan! ♥" The yelling turned into a shriek of delight, and Airi was swallowed up by the wave of puppies.

Seeing her, Yosho was relieved.

"Um..."

"What?!" Beyond the screen was a girl about the same age as Airi when they first met, staring at Yosho, misty-eyed.

"Um, I..." the girl mumbled faintly.

"Excuse me, who are you?" Yosho could not remember her, no matter how he tried.

"Pleased to meet you, Father."

"Huh...?" After his outcry, Yosho's mind went blank.

"I'm your daughter, Minaho!" The girl shyly bowed.

EPILOGUE

Yosho's mouth gaped as understanding dawned upon him, and his lips gradually widened into a smile. "Ha ha ha..."

Why was Airi, who had returned to Airai, now at the Academy? Who knew what had happened in these one hundred-plus years? But deep in Yosho's subconscious, he had the feeling that those difficult but fun and boisterous days would return.

THE END

Afterword

It's been eight years (though it may be longer, as my memory around here is hazy) since I got involved in the world of *Tenchi Muyo! Ryo-Ohki*. What began with the OVA (original video anime) expanded to a couple TV series, movies, manga, novels, and even video games. Looking back, I'm quite impressed at how far we've come.

All the various players created *Tenchi* in their own way, and what was once derived from a single work has become colossal, but *Tenchi* can be broadly divided into the OVA world that I was involved in, and the world seen in the TV series.

While true that the bulk of it belongs in the TV world, the OVAs also contain just as much backstory (why am I boasting?). Sadly, because of the nature of OVAs, there aren't as many episodes on the same scale as a TV series. Though that meant a high degree of quality could be maintained, the amount of backstory that didn't see the light of day kept accumulating.

"If you see one, assume there are thirty more." It's not that they were like cockroaches, but I had to do something about them… It was constantly in my thoughts. Then one day, in the height of the summer heat, on my way home by bicycle from a recording studio about forty minutes away from home, I stopped at Orphee (the studio where Kuroda-kun works). Kuroda-kun had been sleeping after finishing up work, so I basically woke him up and (consequently) made him chat with me until the wee hours of the next morning. The topic of novelizing the backstories came up, and that was how the project was born.

The title at the time was supposed to be *New Tenchi Muyo!*, but while the novelization got delayed for some reason or another, the same title was used for a TV series, so the "Shin" (New) became "Shin" (True). (If only I hadn't been someone who worried about public image… we would've named it something like the *Original Tenchi Muyo!* or the *Authentic Tenchi Muyo!*, like a cheesy souvenir shop at a tourist destination or some noodle shop… There's a twinge of regret.)

Anyway, thanks to Kuroda-kun, who patiently stuck with me, *True Tenchi Muyo!* is in its second volume. Yosho finally got to Earth, with Ryoko safely locked up in the shrine, in this book that was written as interpolation from the OVAs, and to start a domino effect of delivering backstory. But then, as you could tell from reading, all but the most necessary events were abridged. It was supposed to be a domino effect, but for space and composition purposes, a lot of the dominoes were left untouched. Well, one day they'll branch off into their own dominoes (perhaps leaving orphans of their own) but, with this volume, the Jurai arc is finished.

AFTERWORD

I'm pretty sure most of the questions from the OVAs have been answered. The stories of what happened to Airi and how Tenchi's parents met (in *True Tenchi*, his mother's name is going to be Kiyone) will have to wait for another time; the next volume will focus on another big mystery, the Washu arc.

We touched on it a little bit in this book in the form of Seto's report, but it's the story of Washu and Akara Naja, the friend who was a major influence on her, and how they met, Washu's marriage and childbirth... and separation... It will take place not in the Galaxy Academy but back when it was called the Jurai Imperial Academy. Please look forward to it.

—Kajishima Masaki

APOLOGY

We boasted in the conversation at the end of *True Tenchi Muyo! Volume One: Jurai* that we would "meet again in the afterword interview for Volume Two," but it turns out that due to various circumstances, there won't be an interview this time. I apologize to everyone who had been looking forward to Kajishima Masaki and Kuroda Yosuke's Big Show. I'm sure it will resume in Volume Three, so please look forward to it.

—Kuroda Yosuke

True Tenchi Muyo!

Character Sheets

ARTWORK BY KAJISHIMA MASAKI

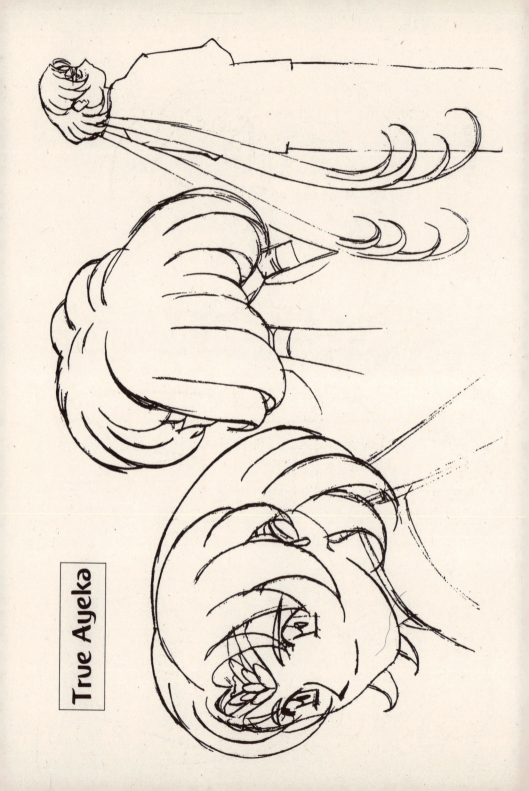

True Ayeka

Masaki Ayeka
(TODDLER)

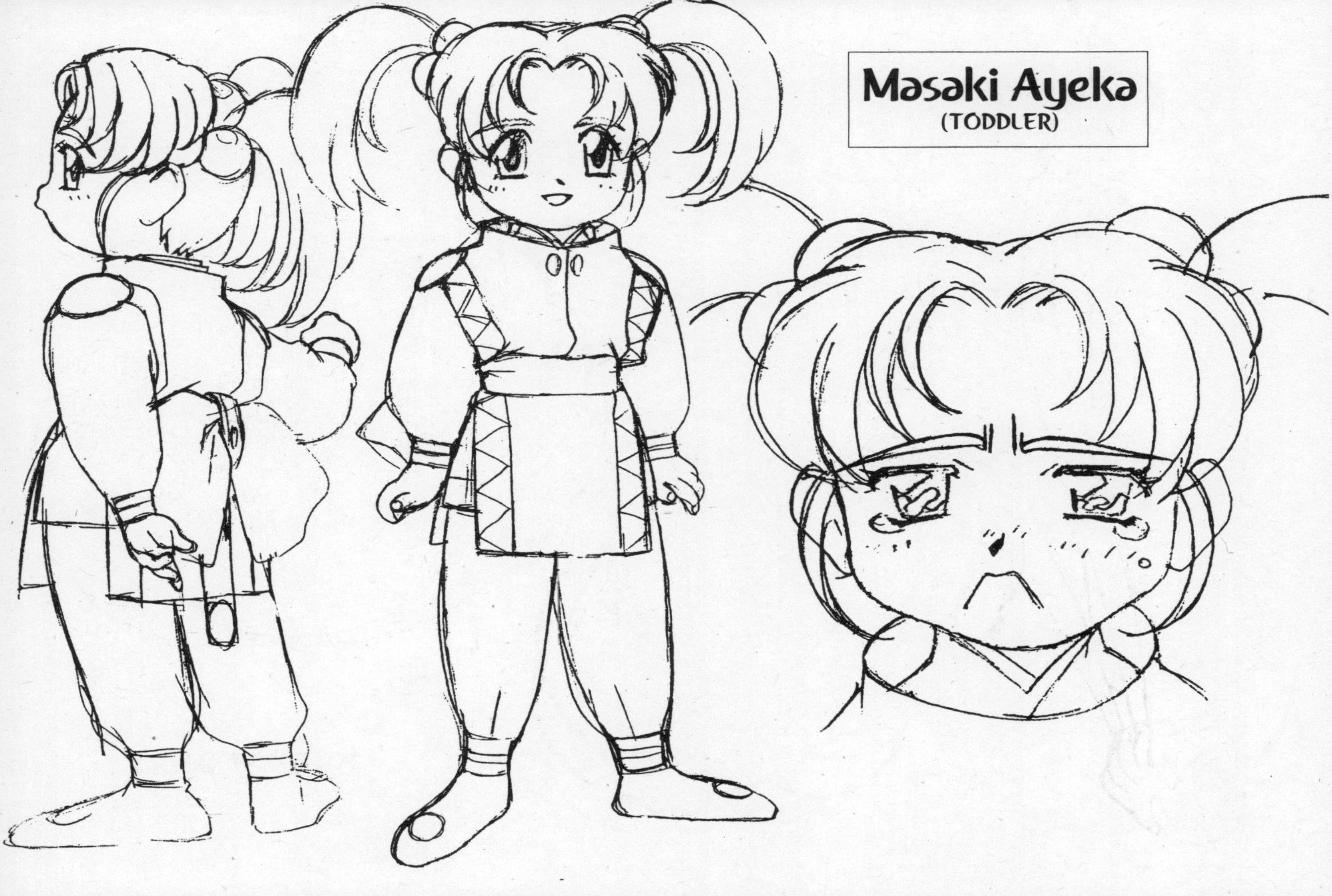

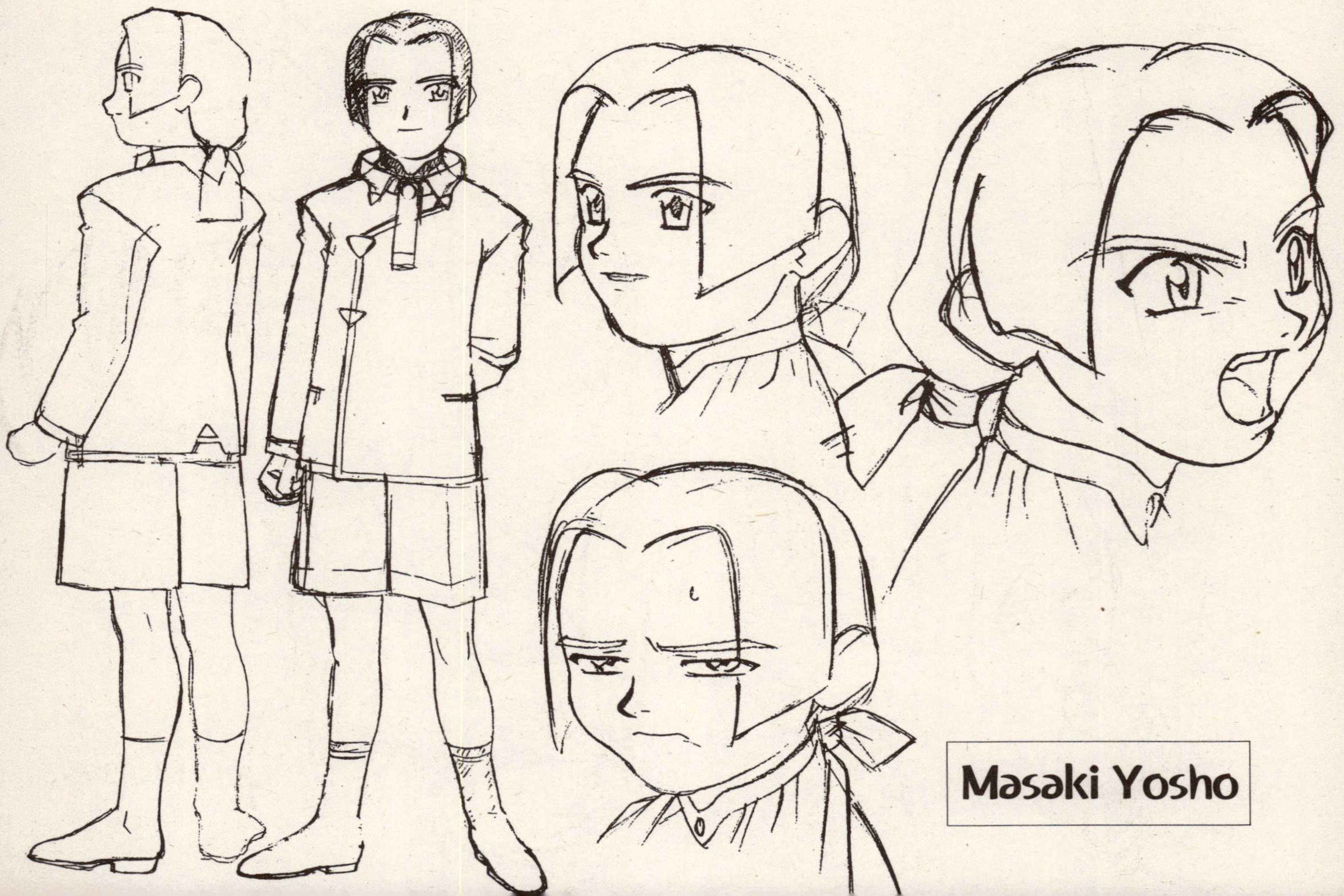
Masaki Yosho

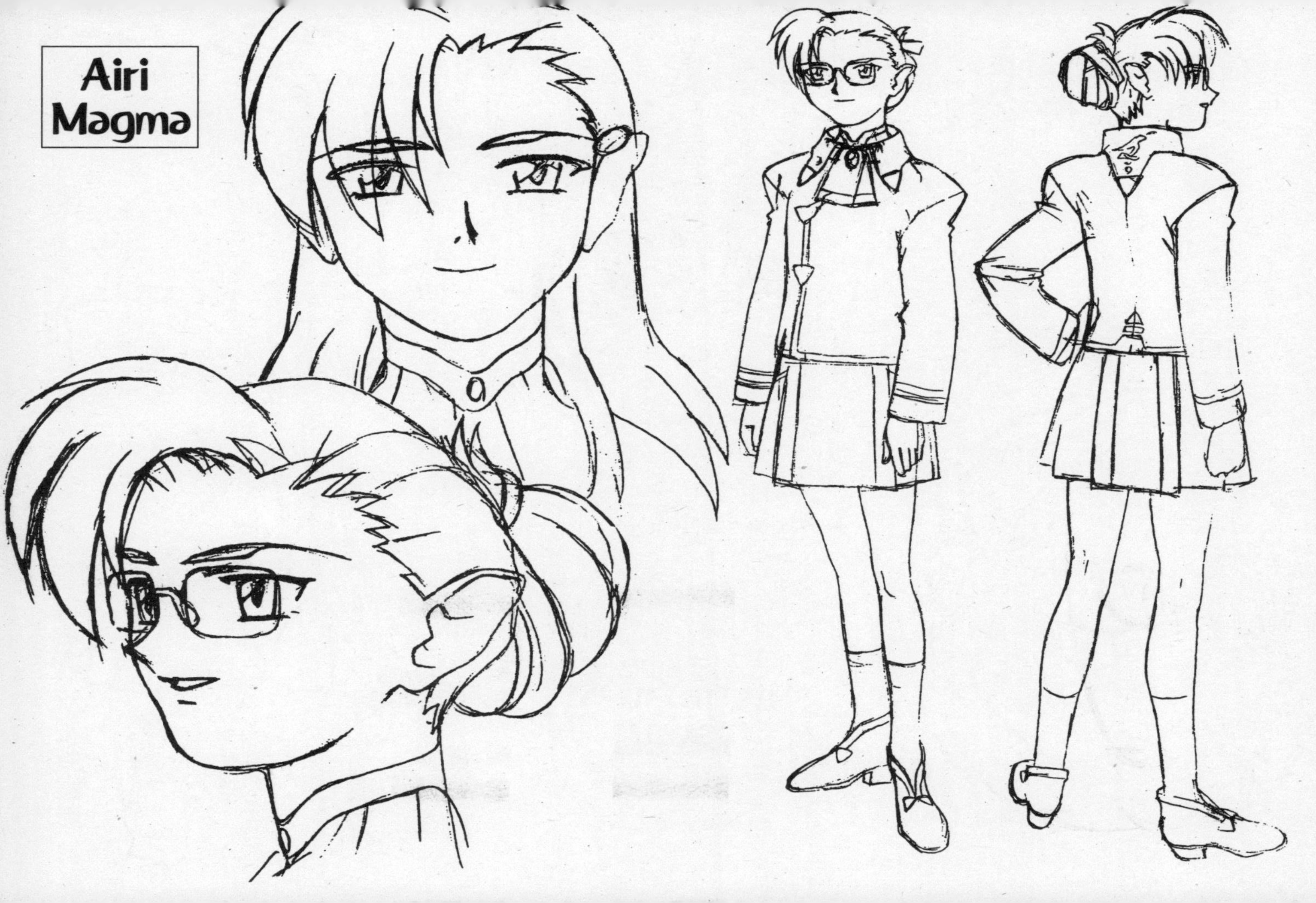
Airi
Magma

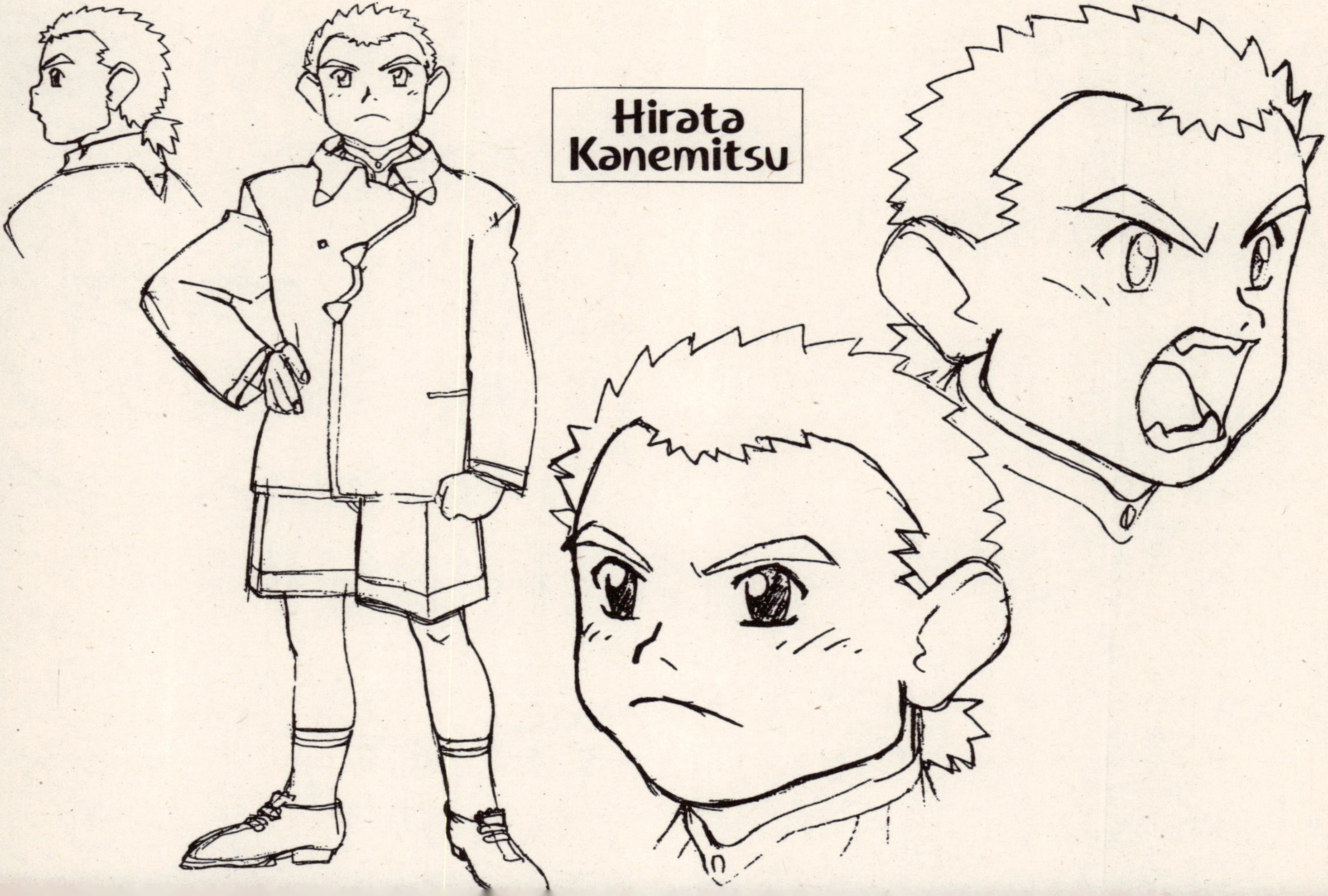
Hirata
Kanemitsu